EL Porto Summer

A YA Novel By
George Matthew Cole

Chapter 1

Brett Sloan's long, muscled, taut, teenage body stirred. In his dream, a bikini-clad girl was staring at him. Her hypnotic, violet eyes were offset by short, jet-black hair and a cream-colored complexion. Brett was hypnotized by the stunning vision facing him. The sexy girl whispered as she floated closer.

"Would you like me to remove my top?"

Surprised by this offer, Brett reached out to touch her but could not grasp anything physical. He opened his eyes to see his empty hands reaching toward the bedroom ceiling. *There she goes again. Another disappearing dream girl,* he thought.

Brett wiggled his toes at the end of his six foot plus body, which extended about two inches over the end of the bed. He pulled himself halfway up and stopped. As he began to wake up, he remembered what day it was and his young face broke into a grin. It was the first day of summer! He plopped back down and luxuriated in the knowledge that there was no reason to hurry and no special place he had to be. The usual list, in his head, of important things to accomplish, had disappeared. Still only half awake, he remembered watching the Johnny Carson show late into the night. *Now that summer vacation's here, I can take my time. No hurrying around to do stuff I don't care about anyway.*

Muted sunlight crept around the edges of the thick curtains that covered the one window in his small bedroom. *Well, it looks like it's sunny out there,* he thought. Brett envisioned his life for the next three months. This was what he lived for. Summer was the ultimate experience for a sixteen-year-old who lived at the beach in Southern California. *Surfing, bodysurfing, biking on The Strand, babe-watching, or just hanging out; I can do anything I want.*

Brett pulled on a T-shirt and headed toward the kitchen of the small two-bedroom apartment. He lived with his mother Ann. The

1

apartment, which also had a small front living room, a tiny den and a small kitchen, was neat and clean, except for Brett's room. His bedroom was for sleeping and his mother had given up on the idea of her son keeping it tidy. Ann, a waitress, was already at work. Brett was on his own. He quickly ate a bowl of cereal with black coffee and then jumped into the shower. He started to anticipate a sunny day at the beach. As the streams of water hit him, he thought of lying in the sun and frolicking in the surf. *I better get out of this shower and see what the ocean looks like. Maybe there are some good surfing waves.*

Brett Sloan lived in El Porto. El Porto was the ten blocks on the northern end of Manhattan Beach, California. Highland Avenue ran north and south high above the Pacific Ocean. Long, steep hills sloped down from Highland Avenue to the clean, sand beach in front of the cement walkway known as The Strand. The Strand was a main conduit in the summer and a center of activity. A short bank eased down to a parking lot. Lifeguard towers and the occasional volleyball court dotted the beach below. Thin two-story homes lined the steep, narrow streets with names like Kelp and Moonstone. Numbered streets ran between.

Brett stood outside his apartment near the top of Kelp Street. It was late in June, and surprisingly, at least to outsiders, the sky was overcast, causing the air to be cool and damp. Brett wore swimming trunks, flip-flops and a T-shirt. He shivered slightly with a look of disgust on his young, slightly tan, cherubic face. Although his hair was brown now, as the summer progressed it would become blond from exposure to the sun's rays. He was looking down at a bank of fog that came halfway up the hill. *Crap, this is BS. Its summer and I get gray skies and fog. Man, when is this weather going to warm up? It's been like this for three days. I bet the surf's crap too.* Brett shook his head and went back into the apartment. As he changed into warmer clothes the phone rang. He rushed to answer.

"Hello," said Brett.

"Hey dude. It's Greg. What's happinin'?" said a loud enthusiastic voice.

Brett smiled when he recognized who was on the line. Greg and his younger brother Bobby were Brett's best friends. Greg was his age and Bobby was two years younger. He had known them since he moved to El Porto five years earlier. Brett became optimistic about the day to come. He always had a good time with the Stephens brothers.

"Hey man. The day looks like crap. I was just thinking about checking out the surf. I can't believe how cold it is," whined Brett.

"Dude, don't bother. I already checked and it isn't pretty. And the fog makes it so you can't see anything. The surf's flat. Like no waves at all,"

"I guess we need to figure out something else to do. But, what?"

"Do you have any money?"

"Yeah, I think I have about thirty bucks stashed in my room. It's my summer money."

"Bring twenty and come to the house. I know something we can do. You, me and little Bobby. It will be great," crowed Greg.

"What is it?"

He was thinking that twenty dollars was a lot of money, at least to him.

"Just dress warm and come down to the house. And, bring the twenty."

"Okay, I'll see you in about ten minutes," said Brett.

~~~

Brett looked up at a large two-story light blue house facing the Pacific Ocean. It was situated on a prime spot right facing The Strand with an unobstructed view of the Pacific Ocean. *Man, what a house. I sure wouldn't mind living here. Their dad must make the big bucks to be able to pay for this.* The door opened before he knocked. A shorter and heavier, teenager stood facing Brett. Greg Stephens smiled with a twinkle in his brown eyes. He wore Levi's jeans and a sweatshirt with Converse tennis shoes.

"Hey Dude. Come on in. I have a surprise for you.   go in the rec room," said Greg.

"What's the big secret? I brought my twenty bucks," asked Brett.

They walked to the spacious recreation room. Brett noticed the entertainment center and pool table. The television was on. *This room is half as big as our apartment*, thought Brett. Bobby was sitting on a large plush sofa watching television. Unlike his older brother, he was thin bordering on skinny. His freckles stood out under his olive eyes and light brown hair. Brett plopped down on the couch next to Bobby.

"Hey Bobby. How's it goin'? What's Greg cooked up for us?"

"Hell if I know. He doesn't tell me anything. He just said we were doing something."

Both boys looked at Greg who had the television remote in his hand. Greg grinned and casually clicked off the TV. He faced Greg and Bobby.

"Dudes, the surf is flat and it's dark and cold. What are we going to do with ourselves? Just what could make our day fun?" said Greg.

"What big brother? What could make our day fun?" said Bobby.

"I've got us an airplane trip lined up," gushed Greg.

Greg grinned and continued.

"Our neighbor Robert needs help paying for gas so he can get air hours. We're going to Catalina Island and back. How does that sound to you guys?"

"Whoa, awesome" said both teenagers at the same time.

"We walk over to Robert's house in an hour to drive to the airport. We pay ten bucks apiece and hop in a plane and fly to Catalina. This will be a great way to get un-bored.

"Why did I need twenty bucks?" asked Brett.

"We will have lunch at the airport over there. I don't know how much it will be. I guess it's some café or something."

"Man, this is better than waiting around for the sun to come out," said Brett.

Greg paused and thought for a moment.

"Yeah, way better than being bored. You know Brett, I just thought of something. It seems like every girl I talk to these day asks me about you. They always want to know if you have a girlfriend," said Greg

"Why would I want to complicate my summer with a girlfriend? It's like having a ball and chain around your leg," answered Brett.

"Yeah, I tell them you don't have one. But, if you wanted one, there are a lot of candidates."

"Whatever," said Brett.

The three excited teenagers talked about what it would be like to fly over the ocean, what the airplane might look like and other trip related topics. The conversation continued in the old, dilapidated sedan that they rode in. Robert, drove unnoticed while the three teenagers talked in the back. After riding a few miles inland the overcast skies cleared, bringing a sense of optimism to the group. Even the non-talkative pilot said something.

"This is good. It will be a lot better flying with some sunlight. We'll be at the airport in about ten minutes. This will be a lot of fun for you guys," said Robert.

After arriving and seeing the tiny four seat airplane with one small propeller, the teenagers were surprised and a little nervous.

"Wow! That thing is tiny. Will it hold all of us?" asked Brett.

"I've flown commercial but never on one of these," said Bobby.

After they were all situated in the tiny vehicle with Greg sitting in the front and seat belts buckled, they started down the runway. Soon, Robert floored it causing the light plane to accelerate, pushing the boys back into their seats. When they lifted from the runway, it was barely noticeable. The small airplane steadily rose into the air and turned toward the Pacific Ocean which was clearly visible under the bright June sun.

Brett absorbed this new experience. *Man, this thing feels like it's made out of rubber bands and Popsicle sticks. Those buildings and cars down there are like little toys. Totally unreal, man, totally.* Robert talked a little bit about the steps he needed to obtain his flying license. He needed a certain number of hours, in the air, to qualify. After a time the boys relaxed a bit as they adjusted to a different kind of flying. Brett looked down at the ocean and saw a large school of fish. The silvery mass just beneath the surface, moved as one organism in complete synchronicity. The sunlight flashed from the amorphous mass, as it twisted and turned. *Now, this is smooth flying. The way I like it*, thought Brett.

Brett's composure was soon interrupted by a change in direction. They were now pointed up and rising quickly. *What the hell is this? I just got comfortable.* He noticed Bobby grabbing on and looking somewhat pale. His lips seemed to be clamped together by invisible vises. Brett sensed that unlike on an airliner, the separation between passengers and the elements was paper thin. He felt like he could punch a hole in the side of the tiny plane with no difficulty. They continued their steep climb until Robert glanced back at them with a mischievous glint in his eyes. Then it happened. The lone engine on the plane stopped, causing it to pause in midair and hover for an instant.

In the front seat Greg said "Uh oh."

God damn it. I knew this was a bad idea as soon as I saw this tin can, thought Brett.

The little engineless box slowly turned sideways toward the blue sea below and fell. It was as if a large crane had picked up a compact car and dropped it. All of the boys feared that their short lives would be over soon. They gasped but said nothing.

"Okay, here we go," said Robert.

He pushed something on the dashboard and the engine of the plane sputtered. He tried to again with the same result. The boys turned white with fear. Robert adjusted something, pounded hard on the dashboard and hit the switch. This time the engine sputtered twice and started. As he pulled back on the steering wheel, the tiny vehicle leveled. An audible sigh came out of the mouths of the young passengers. The tension dissipated like air oozing out of flat tire. Very soon, with the engine purring, they were cruising toward their destination. The boys said nothing for some time. The silence was broken by Robert who was laughing to himself.

"Are you guys okay? That was a stall. It's part of our training. I thought you might find it interesting," he said.

"You weren't trying to scare us were you?" said Greg in a loud voice.

Brett smiled and looked toward Catalina Island. The small island now seemed very close and very friendly. After an uneventful, soft landing the group ate lunch at the Catalina Café. Brett was pleased that it wasn't too expensive. His appetite was still intact, even after having a churning stomach during the stall. Bobby, who didn't look like he ate much anyway, didn't eat at all but had a Seven-up. He was still pale. His big brother Greg, who looked like he never missed a meal, dug in.

The flight back was routine but the stall maneuver was never far from the thoughts of the young passengers. None of them could forget the feeling of sitting in a tiny box high up in the air, with no engine running and nothing but ocean underneath. The sense of relief was overwhelming when they touched down on the mainland.

I won't forget this trip anytime soon, thought Brett.

Chapter 2

The San Fernando Valley was hot and stifling. Volleyball practice was over. Jane Jones, who was known to her friends as Janey, fidgeted while listening to her volleyball teammates in the back seat of the VW Van. Her quiet, nervous energy and shy personality was in contrast to most of her outgoing, competitive teammates. She fit in well and, in spite of her introverted personality, was a fierce competitor. Her short blond hair with a muted streak of gray topped a svelte, taut, body. She was tall but carried herself with the grace and assurance of an accomplished athlete.

School had been out for a week and Janey was forced to face the inevitable. The brightness in her distinctive blue eyes faded as she envisioned her future. She was moving. She was leaving the only home she had ever known. The temporary escape, while practicing with her best friends, was not enough to stop the feelings of despair that were again assailing her.

Maria Santos, a short, pleasant girl, could see Janey become more despondent with each passing block. The girls talked about the summer, boys and volleyball exploits while Janey sat in silence gazing out the window.

"What's wrong Janey?" asked Maria.

Janey thought for a moment. She could think of nothing that was good or right in her life. It was all wrong. Her future was dark and cold.

"I'm leaving everything. The Valley is all I've ever known. I'll miss you guys," moaned Jane.

"Hey, we won't forget you. We are only a phone call away. And you can visit us or we can visit you," said Maria.

"It will never be the same. I will have a new school, new everything."

"Isn't your cousin there? Won't she help you get settled in?" asked Lori from the front seat.

"Yeah, she's there but I hardly know her. I'm sure of one thing though. She doesn't play volleyball. I think she is boy crazy or something," said Janey.

Maria continued, hoping that Janey would feel better now that they had her talking.

"Speaking of boys, what about Todd? What does he have to say about you moving away?"

Janey looked at Maria, put her hands to her face and started to cry. Nothing was said by anyone for the remainder of the ride.

Janey waved to her friends and walked into her house, a brown rambler. Half opened packing boxes were everywhere. Jane's room looked just like the rest of the house, in a state of transition. To Janey it was like a graveyard in the dead of winter. She flopped on her bed and looked at the ceiling trying not to think about the packing she had to do. The move, the breakup with Todd, the loss of her friends; it was as if the bottom of her bedroom cracked open uncovering an endless abyss of sadness. Janey closed her eyes hoping that it was all a bad dream.

Jane's mother Joann poked her head in the doorway. She wore a T-shirt and shorts. Her dyed blond hair was disheveled and her gray-blue eyes displayed concern for her only child.

"Honey, how are you doing?" asked Joann.

"Not good. Please tell me this is not happening," moaned Jane.

"I'm sorry honey. It is happening and you need to start packing stuff up. And, when you are done here I have a lot more work for you."

"Can't I just hang out for awhile? I don't have any energy," whined Jane.

"You have been avoiding this, but now we are out of time. It will all work out. I know you don't think so, but it will,"

Janey stared at her mother with resentment.

"There's so much crap to pack. Can't we get some help or something?"

"I thought maybe that nice boy Todd could help. He seems like a strong young man."

Janey hopped up from the bed and started working. She turned to her mother.

"Let's just get this over with. And, let's not talk about Todd, ever."

Joann knew from Jane's tone that it was time to exit.

"Okay Janey. Come down when you are done up here."

Janey worked without thought of where things should go or what box to fill. She grabbed each item like it was an enemy and slammed it into whatever open receptacle was nearest. *At least I'll get away from Todd*, thought Janey as she began to cry again.

El Porto Summer

Chapter 3

The three ratty looking teenagers slithered up the steep hill moving slowly toward Highland Avenue. One was tall and overshadowed the other two, who were short and skinny. The three exuded an air of danger and criminality. Passersby would step aside to avoid them. The taller boy had bright red hair. He wore a green and black flannel shirt, flapping over holey blue jeans. Both of his companions wore shorts, flip-flops and dirty T-shirts. The tall one, Jimmy Brooks was the obvious leader and stood out in numerous ways. He walked with determination but in a disjointed style as if some invisible force was causing him to appear like he was an oversized puppet being manipulated by invisible strings. His bobbing pimply-faced head looked alternately side to side as if searching something to steal or somebody to ambush. It was as if none of his body parts, although strong, were properly connected.

It was the end of the day and the sun was setting. Nobody observing the trio would expect them to be up to anything resembling good. They skulked forward like overgrown rodents looking for scraps in dark places. About half way up a very steep El Porto hill, Jimmy put out both of his long, bony arms holding back his partners. He pulled them over to the side of the narrow street.

"Listen up assholes. We need some cash. How much do you have?" said Jimmy.

Both of his companions smiled at the word assholes which was to them a term of endearment. It made them proud even though, to most, it seemed derogatory. The one named Freddy pulled a non-filtered cigarette out of a pack in his T-shirt pocket. Other than his long stringy hair, his most noticeable trait was crooked yellow teeth. He also exuded a lack of physical presence, as if his muscles had not been exercised enough.

"Hey Jimmy. I have a buck and some change. Maybe Dusty has some bucks. What do we need it for?" asked Freddy.

"What about it, Dusty. Got any coin? I have a plan," said Jimmy.

Dusty with short hair and a skull and crossbones tatoo on one of his thin white arms scowled.

"Naw, I ain't got none. I spent it all on smokes and gas," said Dusty.

"Okay, follow me. Maybe I can get some cash at my fucked up pad," said Jimmy.

The three 18-year-olds arrived at the tiny rundown apartment at the north end of El Porto above Highland Avenue, about fifteen minutes later. Before they entered Jimmy gave instructions.

"It looks like my old lady is there with her boyfriend. I know she won't give me anything. You guys keep her talking and I'll see if I can swipe some money," he whispered.

The trio walked into the ground floor apartment with Jimmy in front. The tiny, messy, living room was occupied by a middle-age, heavy-set, red haired women. Her face looked ashen and her puffy eyes were bloodshot. Next to her sat a balding, grim-faced 50ish man who wore a black, short-sleeved Harley Davidson sweatshirt. He had tattoos on both arms. The two were watching an old small, black and white television. The room stank of stale cigarette smoke due to the overflowing ashtrays, sitting on barely discernable tables, mixed with old beer and wine odors. Empty beer bottles were strewn around the room.

Jimmy nodded to his mother and kept walking while the other two boys stopped and started talking at the same time. The man looked up with tense jaws and irritation. Freddy and Dusty were talking at Jimmy's mother but saying little that made sense. Jimmy's mother, Cora was in no condition to answer and just stared ahead through glazed eyes. Jimmy stopped in the kitchen. He knew he had little time before his mom's biker boyfriend got mad enough to pull himself up and do something. He lifted the lid to a cookie jar and found about a dollar's worth of change which he pocketed. He then slipped into his mother's dingy, bedroom and grabbed her purse. He quickly rifled through it finding one five dollar bill. On his way back to the front room, he leaned into the bathroom and flushed the toilet. In the living room Jimmy looked at his inebriated mother.

"I just had to pee," he said.

She said nothing but took another drink of beer.

The boyfriend glared at Jimmy.

"Get the hell out of here. Can't you see we're busy? Go mug a cop or something."

"Screw you and your biker friends. I live here too. Let's go boys," said Jimmy.

"You keep giving me crap and you will be out on the street," said the boyfriend.

But, the three urchins were gone into the early night.

~~~

El Porto Liquor, situated on Highland Avenue in the middle of El Porto, was the main seller of alcohol for all of El Porto. Its stock on hand was extensive and varied. The neon sign above the door, beckoned to the world, making a loud garish statement that its mission in life was to help the public become obtain booze. Jimmy, Dusty and Freddy loitered around the corner waiting for a willing liquor store customer to agree to buy them alcohol. They had already been in the liquor store to stock up on cigarettes but needed help obtaining booze. Jimmy saw a twenty-something guy walking toward the store.

"Hey mister. Could you do me a favor?" asked Jimmy.

He was acting as nice as he could, considering how out of character it was.

"Uh, what?" replied the stranger with a bit of suspicion in his voice.

"We were wondering if you could buy us some beer. We have money."

"What's in it for me?" said the now interested man.

"We just need two of the big bottles of Colt 45. You can have the rest of the money. We have seven bucks," said a hopeful Jimmy.

"Okay, give me the money."

The stranger went into the store as the teenage punks watched. After a short time they became restless.

"If this guy tries to screw us out of our money, we jump him. Got it?"

"Yeah, he can't fuck with us," said Freddy. "It's three to one."

Dusty's eyes got bigger and he started to shiver a little, even though it was a pleasant 75 degrees.

"Alright, here he comes with big bags. I think we're in business," said Jimmy.

The man handed the bags with the two large bottles of Colt 45 to Jimmy.

He said "This stuff is strong. It's nasty too. Are you sure you want this much?" the man asked.

"Oh don't worry. We aren't going to drink it all. Some is for my mom," Jimmy lied. "Thanks mister."

Now that the desired stout malt liquor had been acquired, the trio had a spring in their step, as they walked in the direction of Jimmy's apartment.

"Are we going to our spot?" asked Dusty.

"Yeah, it's good they haven't finished yet. The spot's still safe," answered Jimmy.

After walking for about fifteen minutes the houses started to thin out opening to an area under construction. The boys turned up a dirt driveway and disappeared into the darkness. They all stopped and looked back to check the street, before proceeding to the unfinished house at the end of the driveway. In the back they slipped into the large crawl space underneath. After crawling to a corner away from the entrance, they sat down. Jimmy pulled out a cigarette and lit it up. He rooted around looking for something while the match was still lit.

"Ouch, goddamn match. Someone find the fuckin' candle," growled Jimmy.

Freddy and Dusty rooted around in the dark for a few minutes. Then Dusty lit a match. He touched the match to a candle in his hand. Then he found another and did the same. The illumination revealed three sleeping bags, some eating utensils and plastic cups. Particles of smelly dust created a thick cloud around and on the teenagers. The dust hung in the air refusing to settle to the ground. There were also old, partly torn, Playboy magazines lying in a pile.

Jimmy grabbed a dirty plastic cup and one of the bottles of booze. He turned the twist-off cap and poured. Foam started to overflow the cup which Jimmy hastily shoved at Dusty. Dusty grabbed the flimsy plastic cup but the excess foam spilled onto his pants.

"Crap. Why did you do that? Now, I smell like beer," crowed Dusty.

"Fuck you Dusty. Nobody cares anyway," said Jimmy.

Dusty said nothing but frowned and started to sip his half-full plastic cup of Colt 45. Jimmy with a cigarette dangling from his mouth, poured for himself and Freddy. After a few cups of booze with some cigarettes the demeanor of the group changed from sneaking, scrounging rats to blustery bullies. They alternated between talking about how tough they were and the big crimes they had committed.

"Remember when we pounded that stupid surfer. He never saw it comin'. With three of us to do the hitting, it was easy," said Freddy.

Dusty remembered hitting the helpless surfer and the red blood that seeped out of his wounds. His stomach became queasy. Jimmy's glazed eyes stared into space. His lower lip curled into a snarl.

"I hate surfers. I hate the water and I hate fuckin' surfboards. That wimp deserved what he got," slurred Jimmy.

As he always did when thinking about surfers, Jimmy recalled almost drowning in the ocean as a young boy. When a lifeguard finally dragged him up to the beach, a group of surfers were laughing hysterically. The hatred of that moment was never far from Jimmy's thoughts.

"Yeah man, we got him good," said Dusty.

As the group drank and smoked, Dusty and Freddy seemed to become content and sleepy. But, Jimmy rambled on loudly about what he considered daring exploits, such as stealing from homes in broad daylight, when the owners were away at work, or jumping unsuspecting local kids and taking their money.

"Yeah I even screwed the idiot cops when they took me in. My lawyer got me out. I sat in the tank waiting and nobody there was as tough as me. They just were stupid asses. I got out, with no problem. "

Dusty had been listening in a drunken stupor. His glazed eyes now looked down at his wet shorts. Freddy laughed at him and pointed.

"He peed his pants. Ha, ha, ha," yelled Freddy.

Dusty took awhile to understand what the laughing was about. After it dawned on him, his face became red.

The booze was having a powerful affect on Dusty who felt braver than usual.

"Screw you Freddy. Jimmy spilled this shit on me. Fuckin' Jimmy did it. I didn't pee on nothin'," screamed Dusty.

"Ha, ha, ha, Dusty peed, Dusty peed. Ha, ha," crowed Freddy.

Now Jimmy started to laugh too. He seemed very amused to see Dusty so upset.

"Poor little Dusty," teased Jimmy.

"You're both assholes. Go to hell," yelled Dusty.

In an instant Jimmy leaned over and swung at Dusty who was looking at Freddy. His punch landed on Dusty's cheek with a loud crrraaaccck? Dusty started swinging with a full glass of Colt 45 in one of his hands. Arms flailed and beer flew in all directions. By mere dumb, drunken luck he hit Freddy in the arm and Jimmy on the nose. Jimmy's nose started to bleed and he grabbed Dusty by the shoulder. He began swinging at his face furiously. Because of his drunken state, and the excruciating pain from his bloody nose, most of Jimmy's punches were missing their target. Dusty, who now feared for his life, grabbed a handful of dirt and threw it in Jimmy's face. Jimmy stopped and attempted to clear the dust out of his eyes.

"Ah, ow, you little fucker," yelled Jimmy.

Dusty kept throwing dirt while he scrambled away toward the exit. After about ten yards he turned over and crawled as fast as he could until he was out from under the house and swallowed up by the night.

Chapter 4

It was early evening. Brett and his mother Ann were both anticipating dinner. For her it was a chance to be with her son. For him it was the desire to feed a huge appetite. The small black and white television set that sat directly in front of the living room couch, was not behaving itself. Brett frowned while he fiddled with the rabbit ear antenna on the top of the small square box. The old, tired, television, alternately displayed snow, a flipping diagonal line, and occasionally, a clear picture. After finding a position to receive a relatively clear signal, he plopped down on the couch and watched "The Dating Game".

Ann was in the small kitchen cooking hamburgers on top of the stove while French fries roasted in the oven. Although there was a small fan humming, the smoky aroma from the greasy burgers and fries permeated the kitchen and adjacent living room. Ann wore a light, blue, flowered apron over her slim, 37-year-old figure. Worry lines ran next to bright brown eyes, above a resolute mouth. Her medium length hair was a shiny auburn color. As she prepared dinner, a smile came to Ann's lips and the worry lines seemed less pronounced.

The living room was tiny, like all the rooms in this well-used two-bedroom apartment. Narrow stairs led up to their second story home near the top of Kelp St. The two-apartment building was tightly wedged between two other narrow homes. The furniture within was worn from years of use. Ann, who possessed an abundance of nervous energy, kept the apartment neat, clean and cozy.

Ann smiled as she thought about how lucky she was. After the divorce, it was difficult, but she and Brett had survived without losing their home. Her income from waitressing, along with the checks from Brett's father in Palm Springs, was just enough to pay for rent and other necessities. Although Brett did not have as much as most of his friends, Ann knew how much her son loved being near the beach and ocean. Although Brett had mentioned getting a job, Ann wanted her son to enjoy what was left of his childhood. Also, she feared that a job would distract him from schoolwork and that was not going to happen if she could stop it. After sitting in the middle of a cloud of greasy hamburger fumes for some time, Brett's stomach began to growl. He peeked into the kitchen hoping that it was time to eat.

"Mom, is it done yet?" said Brett

Almost honey. Wash your hands and come to the table"

Brett did as he was told. At the kitchen table, Brett saw and smelled the cheeseburger and fries on his plate. The food caused his mouth to water and his stomach to growl again. He attacked his first cheeseburger as if he had not eaten in days. He said nothing while inhaling his food.

"Brett, slow down," said Ann.

"Sorry Mom. I was really starving."

"Tell me what you have been doing."

"Nothing much. Greg and Bobby want me to go to Disneyland with them. I spent most of my money on the airplane ride though."

Ann frowned at the mention of the airplane ride. She knew Brett was usually good about keeping her informed but sometimes acted without remembering. Since his dad exited their lives, Brett had become more and more independent.

"You have to ask me first when you go off flying with strangers. Don't do that again," scolded Ann.

"Yeah, I know. But, I get excited and forget stuff," said Brett.

"Who is taking you kids to Disneyland? And when is it supposed to happen?"

"Oh, Mrs. Stephens is taking us, if I can go. I think they want to go later this week."

"I'll see if I can find some extra money. Maybe I will get some good tips. I'll call over there to see what's going on.

19

"Thanks Mom," said Brett.

A light came into Ann's eyes causing Brett to take notice. He could almost see little wheels turning behind her pretty face.

"You know Brett. I was just wondering?" she said.

"Yeah."

"Are any girls going with you to Disneyland? I answer the phone sometimes with giggling girls on the line."

"No girls mom. Don't get me wrong. I like girls, but I don't want to date or any of that stuff."

"Well you know that someday you might want a girlfriend. And, I think there will be plenty of girls who want you for a boyfriend, too."

Brett looked at his mother with a bit of anger in his eyes.

"I tried the girlfriend thing in 8th grade. I didn't like it. She called me all the time and tried to control my life. When I didn't want to be with her every minute, she told her friends I didn't like her anymore. I don't want that again. No way."

Ann's bright eyes twinkled.

"Brett. You are getting old enough that you might want to keep an open mind about girls. They may be hard to avoid," said Ann with a knowing look.

"Whatever you say Mom, but I don't think I will change my mind."

Ready to leave the talk about girls behind, Brett started thinking about Disneyland and all of the things he liked about going there. Ann noticed his attention was far away and remembered another topic that she wanted to discuss.

"One more thing, Brett. When does summer school start?"

"Oh, uh, yeah. It starts in about a month. What a drag," moaned Brett.

"Honey, you know how important that is. You need to keep your grades up to get into college," said Ann.

"Yeah, I know it's important. But, it's in the summer, the worst time," whined Brett.

"You need to concentrate and do the work. If you had done it before you wouldn't have to attend summer school," said his mother sternly.

Brett finished his second cheeseburger and fries and went back to watching TV. He did not focus on the TV as his thoughts alternated between girls, school and the myriad attractions of summer. *Dammit! Summer will just be getting good when I have to go to that stupid summer school. At least I have a little time until it starts. I'll deal with it later,* he thought.

Brett heard his mother talking on the phone and knew that she was talking with Mrs. Stephens about the Disneyland trip. Thoughts of school and girlfriends disappeared as he saw himself walking around The Magic Kingdom. *This is going to be great. And, I get to go with my best friends.* Although he had visited Disneyland many times, he never tired of it. As he filled his head with visions of rides and castles he smiled and thought, *I don't care if there aren't any waves and the sun isn't shining. Now, the summer can start.*

Chapter 5

The tiny Chevrolet Corvair pulled up in front of a light, blue, split-level tract home in the sleepy town of El Segundo, California. Joann Jones stared ahead with dead-fish eyes as her daughter Janey wiped away tears. The sixteen-year-old turned away from her mother as she began to speak.

"Honey, I know you don't want to be here, but it can't be helped. This is the best teaching job I could find. We need both your dad and I to work to make ends meet," said Joann.

Janey refused to turn her head to face her mother. She stared at her new home with dread.

"Mom, I still can't believe you are doing this to me? I'm going to be a sophomore. All my friends are back home in the Valley. I don't know anybody here."

"Janey, come on. You know your cousin Stacy. Her mom told me that Stacy was really excited that you were moving here. And, you will meet people playing volley ball. You aren't usually like this. Where did my strong, brave, athletic, little girl disappear to?"

"I haven't been a little girl for a long time," snapped Janey, who now turned and glared at Joann.

"Janey, I can't see why you are so upset. You knew this was coming."

Janey sat in the car and remembered her life in The Valley. It seemed like a long time since life was normal and she was standing on solid ground. She flashed back to her short relationship with Todd Benson. It was her first deep, emotional romance but ended with Janey having a broken heart. To Janey, everything seemed to be going so well. Todd liked volleyball and her friends. It was easy to be with him and he didn't push her. They had kissed extensively. When things got a little too hot, Todd did not force Janey to go beyond her intimacy comfort zone. She was beginning to feel safe and connected to Todd. Her world was complete when he was with her. The fact that she was moving did not change her feelings at all. She just did not think about how it would work out. She just knew that it would. Janey did notice that Todd had not been calling as much but she had been busy. Then her world crashed around her. She was looking in store windows at the mall, with a girlfriend, when she saw Todd. At first she was excited to see him but then Alison Reed walked up and put her arm around Todd. Next, she kissed his cheek. Janey gasped and clenched her teeth, causing her friend to look at her in surprise. As Janey watched, Todd smiled and turned toward Alison. He kissed her on the lips. When Janey saw Alison open her mouth, she turned away and ran leaving her stunned girlfriend looking around in wonder. Janey lived for days in the middle of an emotional storm. As she made up yet another excuse for Todd's actions something unusual happened. It was as if another person appeared inside her head. That person was practical and little steely. Now, in spite of her yearnings and fears, she decided to call Todd and deal with whatever happened.

"Do you still like me?" asked Janey

"Uh, yeah, I like you. Why do you say that?" asked Todd.

"So, you aren't doing anything with other girls?"

There was a hesitation on the end of the line.

"Er, like what?"

"Like hugging and kissing Alison at the mall," hissed Jane.

"Uh, you saw me at the mall? That's no big deal. We're just friends. Anyway, you'll be moving soon. So, I figured it was okay," said Todd.

"And why is it okay?"

"Well, we can't really go steady if you are living somewhere else, can we?"

Janey hung up the phone with the realization that some people adjusted to life changes differently than others. Her logical side knew that Todd was right. They could not be together after she moved. But her teenage emotions erupted in a cascade of tears.

I'll never fall in love again, she thought, *never, never, never.*

After returning to the present, Janey opened the door of the tiny compact car and un-scrunched her trim, athletic body. She pulled herself up and out. Still crying she ran to the house. Her mother's eyes also glistened. Janey slammed the door behind her and faced stacks of boxes. She kicked a stack knocking it over. A medium sized, pleasant man, with a full head of jet black hair, came out of the kitchen as she started up the stairs to the top floor.

"Janey, wait," said Don Jones.

Janey turned with a scowl on her face. Slight streaks of makeup splotched her cheeks.

"Dad, I don't want to talk now," she said.

Don Jones quickly walked to his daughter and hugged her.

"Pumpkin, I know this is hard for you. I'm here if I can help," he said.

Janey looked at him with the eyes of a ten-year-old rather than those of the sixteen-year-old that she was. Her fierce demeanor of just minutes earlier was now gone and replaced with by helplessness and angst.

"Oh Daddy, I'm so not able to talk now. I need to be alone," said Janey as she scurried up the stairs.

"Janey, Stacy called. She sounded like she really wants to talk to you," called the hopeful father as his daughter disappeared around the corner.

~~~

Stacy Small sat in her bedroom. Teddy bears and other stuffed animals were strewn across the large bed. Pink walls and fluffy curtains created an aura of extreme girlishness. Stacy wore fitted blue jeans and a purple blouse with light blue ruffles running down the front. Her long Black hair accented a tanned face and brown, overly, made-up eyes. A few scattered pimples peeked out from under her makeup. Stacy picked up a pink princess phone and dialed. Janey answered her private line.

"Hello, who's this," said Jane.

"Hi, Janey. This is Stacy," said a singsong voice.

"Oh hi Stace. What's up?"

"Let's get together. Why don't you come over?"

"Er, uh, I'm not feeling so hot. You know just a little down," said Jane.

"Listen, I know it can be tough moving to a new town. You need to get out of that boring old house and cheer up. Come over and we can look at my new bikini and talk about boys," said Stacy.

While Janey thought over her offer, Stacy stood and paced around her bedroom with the phone in her hand. Stacy's face reflected inner plans and schemes. The longer she waited the faster she paced. Finally, she could wait no more.

"Come on. I need some company. We have the summer ahead of us. I need you to help me plan it out. Please, please," Stacy pleaded.

"Okay, I'll ask my dad to drive me over. But I don't want to talk about boys," said Jane.

"No, don't do that. I have my drivers permit. I will drive over with my mom and pick you up. And, we can talk about whatever you want. I promise."

The two cousins sat in Stacy's bedroom. Janey said little while she fidgeted in her chair. She felt like she was sitting in the middle of a huge gob of cotton candy. The entire room made her uncomfortable. The pink décor, piles of makeup and stuffed animals caused her to feel like a reluctant intruder in an alien world. Stacy stood in front of her, wearing a bright red and purple bikini. She was smiling.

"So what do you think?" asked Stacy.

Janey looked at her cousin. Her short, compact, well proportioned, body was tan from head to toe. Her breasts were developed for a young teenage girl and were accentuated by the skimpy bikini top.

"Wow, how did you get that tan already? Summer just started," asked Jane.

"Oh, I used a tanning light. I wanted to get a head start. I can't wait for the sun to show up. What about this cute bikini. How does it look?"

"It looks great. I could never wear something like that. Not with my tiny breasts," said Janey.

"Come on. They aren't that tiny. I think you look great with that athletic body. You don't need to use much makeup like I do. And, you don't have pimples."

"Well I am glad for that but I wonder if I am ever going to develop."

"Janey, I just noticed something. What is that streak in your hair? Is it natural or did you do something to it?

"Um, it's just a gray streak. I've always had it. Mom says I have a hidden temper and that streak is a sign," said Jane.

"What temper? I sure haven't seen it."

"So, do you go to the beach a lot? I never have," asked Jane

"I love the beach. I go whenever I can. You have to come with. It has everything; the sun, the water, the boys. And, I can find out all of the latest news, like who is going with who and all that."

"I hear they play volleyball at the beach?"

"All the time. I see them playing at El Porto every day."

Janey tried to envision what it would be like to be at the beach in El Porto. It was difficult seeing herself in a bathing suit, on the sand in front of boys and even men. But her passion for volleyball, an area of success, was beginning to overshadow her shyness and outright fear. She wondered how her volleyball skills would translate to the way it was played on the beach. *What is it like playing in the sand? How do you fight the hot sun? How many players are on a team?* Although she still had many reservations about stepping onto the sand, now the idea was not as unthinkable. She was happy to see that her cousin knew her way around, too.

"So, do you know a lot of people that go to El Porto?" asked Jane.

"Oh, yeah. Didn't you know? I know everybody. And, I just unloaded my boyfriend. So I'm looking. Really looking."

"Well, I'm not. The last thing didn't work out. Have you had a lot of boyfriends?"

"I've had my share. I get bored easy. What happened with you?" said Stacy.

"He knew I was going to move and just started kissing any girl he could find. I don't think I am very good at the going steady thing. I get really hurt when it doesn't work out," said Janey.

"These high school things don't usually last long. Keep moving forward. There are lots of bitchin' guys out there. You can find one. It's not that hard if you try a little. I'll help."

"I'm not in the mood to try and I don't know if I want any help," said Janey with a slight warning tone in her voice.

Because Stacy was so much her opposite, Janey found herself becoming more comfortable with each passing minute. It became easy for Janey to open up. Stacy seemed to have an answer for every question. Her cousin's obvious social skills and contacts convinced Janey that it would be good to have Stacy as her friend. Cousin Stacy seemed to have everything that she lacked; confidence, friends and a plan. Also, Stacy was such a talker that it was easy for Janey to keep up her side of the conversation.

Chapter 6

Brett sat in the small living room reading a book. It was a novel about Horatio Hornblower, the famous sea captain. *Man, I love the ocean but living on one of those old buckets must have been really bad*, he thought. He heard the front door open as his mother returned from work. She walked into the living room still wearing her waitress uniform. Brett stood up and hugged her. *Man, she works hard every day to support us*, he thought.

"How was work mom?"

"Just another day. I did okay on tips, I guess," said Ann.

Ann sat in a chair facing Brett with a serious look. Brett noticed worry lines and Ann's brown eyes flitted from side to side. *Something up with her, but what?* Brett tried to think of anything that he had done to cause her to be upset.

"I wanted to talk to you about something, Brett," she said.

"Sure,"

"You know I haven't dated much since your dad and I split up. Now, I've been asked out but I'm wondering what to do?"

Brett sensed that his mother was undecided about dating because of him, which came as a surprise. *So, she's asking me about dating. Hmm, I wonder how it will change things?* After thinking about it, Brett guessed that it probably wouldn't have much of an impact on his life. He wasn't going to interfere anyway.

"Whatever, don't worry about me. I just want you to be happy," he said.

"It's okay then? You don't mind?" asked Ann.

"Sure it's okay. You can do what you want. You don't need to ask me."

"Well, he wants to take me out this weekend. So, you be nice when he shows up. His name is Kevin," said Ann.

"Oh, I'll be nice as long as he isn't a dork," kidded Brett with a smile.

Ann sighed with relief.

~~~

It was Friday night. Since Brett had nothing planned he stayed home. Ann, showed up with a pepperoni pizza and a large bottle of pop for Brett. She knew it was his favorite. The aroma of cheese and pepperoni grabbed Brett's attention.

"Oh pizza. What's going on," said Brett.

"Did you forget? I have a date tonight," said Ann.

"Yeah, I knew you had a date on the weekend but you never told me it was tonight,"

"Well, he'll be here soon and I have to get ready. I thought you might like a treat."

She went into her bedroom. Brett wondered what the big deal was but didn't dwell on it. He sat in front of the TV and attacked the pizza. After about thirty minutes Ann came back into the living room.

"Well, I'm ready," she announced.

Brett looked up and was stunned when he saw her. She was wearing a bright purple dress with nylons and high heels. Her face was artfully made up, causing Brett to wonder if this was his mother or some other woman who got lost and walked into their apartment. The entire ensemble was topped off with a string of small white pearls.

"Wow Mom, you look fantastic. This guy is lucky."

"Thanks honey. I don't get to dress up much. So, I am sort of enjoying it. At least I can still remember how."

Brett was still absorbing the new mom he heard a knock on the door. Ann, who was now radiating subtle, frenetic, energy spun and headed toward the front door. Brett heard some muffled words and looked up. Ann came into the living room with a short, neat looking man of about forty, who seemed a bit on edge to Brett. The man wore black slacks and a white shirt. Next to his mother, who now seemed dazzling, the man looked plain and boring.

"Brett, this is Kevin. You don't need to get up," said Ann.

Brett looked up surprised. *I guess I thought the guy wouldn't be so much like a mouse*, he thought.

"Uh, hi. I'm Brett," he said.

Kevin, who was not much taller than his mother, smiled nervously.

"Hello, Brett. It's nice to meet you," he said.

"So what are you guys going to do?" asked Brett.

"We're going to a movie in Hermosa Beach. We're going to the early show. I don't think we'll be that late," answered Ann.

"Okay, have a good one," said Brett.

Ann and Kevin turned and headed for the door. Ann turned toward Brett with a wistful look. She stood for a few moments and then followed Kevin. Brett could not help but feel a bit sorry for his mother. He wanted her to be happy but her date seemed so uninteresting that he wondered if that was possible. *I hope she has a great time. She should have some fun once in a while.*

After eating as much pizza and drinking as much pop as he could handle, Brett sat back and thought about this new development in his life. In spite of attempts to focus his mind on other things, he could not stop thinking about the date. With each passing minute, Kevin seemed more like an enemy who was attacking Brett's territory. The overwhelming emotion, in the teenager's mind, was that of jealousy. *Man, what has gotten into me? It's just one date*, he thought. As much as he tried, he could not help thinking about the connection he had with his mother and how it would be affected by dating and possibly a boyfriend. Various negative thoughts about Kevin kept popping into his mind. Logic told him that there was no good reason for him to see Kevin as an evil intruder, but he could not stop himself. Now that he had seen how attractive his mother could be, he had extreme doubts about Kevin's worthiness. *Why is she going out with that twerp?*

He looks like Mr. boring. She's way out of his league. No wonder he was nervous. He shouldn't even be here.

After battling feelings of anger and jealousy, Brett finally settled down. *I can't do anything about it now, anyway,* he thought. He flipped between channels on the TV until he found a movie to watch. At midnight Brett was ready for bed. He wondered why Ann and her date had not returned, but was too tired to think much about it. He fell into a deep sleep and never heard his mother's return.

The next morning Brett slept in and rolled out of bed in the late morning. He went into the kitchen to grab some coffee. His mother was sitting at the table with a noticeable inner glow. *What the hell? One date and she acts like she's in love,* thought Brett.

"How did last night go?" asked Brett.

"It went better than I thought it would. I think I will be seeing Kevin again."

"Uh, er, uh. You really like that guy? He seemed dorky to me," said Brett not trying to hide his irritation.

"We just hit it off. That's all. Of course it was only one date. I think you should give him a chance. He's really nice," said Ann a bit defensively.

"I'm just surprised. You said you would be home early which didn't happen. And, now you like the guy. He seems really boring to me," said Brett.

Ann sensed her Son's jealousy and was not surprised. She had expected it knowing how close they were. They had weathered the storms together and were bonded for life.

"Let's talk about this some other time. It's not that big of a deal, really," said Ann in a soft voice.

"Okay, Mom. I just want you to be happy. I guess you can date whoever you want. I'm heading out to the beach. I'll see you later."

As Brett put on his swimming suit, he sensed that his mother was trying to fool him into thinking that her date with Kevin was not that important. But he knew his mother well enough that he could tell when she was happy. *If she's happy, why do I feel this way? I should be*

31

happy for her. This whole dating thing is stupid. He let his thoughts wander as he walked down Kelp Street. The glistening ocean beckoned.

Chapter 7

Brett was in a deep sleep and dreaming. In his dream, he was looking at a perfectly formed seven foot high wave coming at him from some distance away. The sun shone behind and through the blue-green, curling water creating a prismatic, kaleidoscopic effect. The slo-motion scene gave him a supreme sense of relaxation and contentment. He started to lean down to paddle his surfboard toward the wave. From a far distance behind him, he heard someone calling. *How can I hear someone calling me from the beach? It's too far away.*

"Brett, dude. Wake up."

Brett became irritated as the perfect wave started to fade away into the sea of his dreamscape. Then, he was moving from side to side and could not cause it to stop. *What the hell is going on?* A loud voice cracked through his sleepy fog.

"Dude, we gotta go. Wake up," boomed the voice.

Brett woke up and tried to get his bearings. The strong embrace of sleep and dreams took a minute to release him. He yawned and looked over at Greg Stephens. Freckle faced Bobby Stephens stood behind his brother looking. Both were laughing like the whole experience was a big joke.

"What's up guys? Man, you screwed up a great dream. What time is it? And what's so funny," mumbled Brett.

"Dude, did you forget? We're going to Disneyland. We're laughing because you looked so pissed off when we woke you up," said Greg.

"Like I said, it was a great dream you guys jumped in the middle of.

Greg yanked the covers off of the bed.

"Get up dude. We came a little early so we could beat the crowds. And, my mom said there will be a big surprise. We have to get going," said Greg

Brett scrambled out of bed and headed toward the bathroom.
He smelled strong coffee aromas coming from the kitchen. He had
to force himself not to detour toward the coffee. After a short time
Brett was showered and dressed in Bermuda shorts, a light blue T-
shirt and low-cut, tan, tennis shoes with no socks.

"Man, how about some of that coffee," asked Brett.

Ann handed him a large thermos and some Styrofoam cups. She
hugged Brett.

"This is for the trip. You kids have a good time. Greg, thank
your mom for me," said Ann.

The three teenagers bounced down the stairs and into the waiting
sedan. The petite, well dressed, Mrs. Stephens sat behind the wheel
of the luxurious, plush Mercedes, automobile. The silver car crawled
up Kelp St. to Highland Avenue and off toward the freeway.

Brett, who was still sleepy, poured a cup of coffee and looked
outside his window at miles of non-descript tract homes next to the
freeway. A haze of smog hung over the inland town with few trees
to be seen. *Man, am I glad I live at the beach*, he thought.

"Mom, how long is it going to take?" asked Bobby.

"Oh, about an hour, honey. You should know that. We've done
this so many times," said his mother in a soft, melodious voice.

"Okay. Oh, and Brett's mom said thanks," said Bobby.

"Hi Brett. How are you doing back there?" asked Mrs. Stephens.

"Uh, I'll be fine once I wake up. Thanks for having me," said
Brett.

"You're welcome. We always like having you come with us."

Brett settled in for the long ride to Anaheim. Anticipation
spurred memories of his Disneyland experiences. He recalled how
the famous, amusement park had changed as he had grown up. One
vivid memory stood out.

Brett remembered riding over Disneyland on the skyway. As he
traveled from Fantasy Land to Tomorrow Land he noticed
construction. The skyway passed through a skeletal structure that
rose into the sky. When complete it would be the Matterhorn

Bobsled ride. Below, the Submarine ride construction was barely started. It was no more than a shallow pit with some metal track laid. *This is my place. It's like home here,* he thought.

The boys started to talk about different experiences at Disneyland.

"One time Bobby got lost. We couldn't find the little dude anywhere," said Greg.

"Yeah, I just asked a guy what to do and he took me to a place for lost kids. Mom and dad showed up after awhile," said Bobby.

"Nothing bad could ever happen inside Disneyland," said Brett.

"Hey Brett. I heard that the seniors are going to have their Senior Party and Prom at Disneyland this year," said Greg.

"For real? That would be awesome. How do they do that?" said Brett.

"They have the party at night. They close it down except for graduating classes from different schools. They all get in for free and can go on any of the rides."

"Man. It makes me want to graduate. No tourists or little gremlins. Not like today," said Brett.

"Yeah, let's get on the best rides before it gets too crowded," chimed in Bobby.

They passed mile after mile of dairy farms. It was a sign to the restless teenagers that they were nearing their destination. Unlike El Porto, the skies were sunny and uplifting. Bobby opened his window allowing a strong flow of air to enter the car. Greg gasped.

"Oh no, stop! Dude, dude, close that window. It smells bad enough with it closed," said Greg.

"Er, uh, yeah. I guess it does," said Bobby putting his thumb and forefinger over his nose.

When the window was closed Bobby said

"I forgot that this is stinky valley. All the cows crap and smell up the place."

"At least it doesn't smell like that at Disneyland," said Brett.

Soon, they saw the top of the Matterhorn and knew they were almost there. The silver Mercedes pulled into the huge parking lot which was about half full. In no time at all the group stood on Main St. Disneyland.

"I know you boys want to get going. Meet me at the riverboat at 12:30. I am going to meet my friend for coffee and chitchat," said Ann.

Greg looked at his mother from behind dark sunglasses.

"Okay Mom. I have a watch and we'll be there. Oh, by the way, what's the surprise?" asked Greg.

"Now, Greg. It wouldn't be a surprise if I told you, now would it?" answered Mrs. Stephens.

"Um, I had to try to find out, didn't I? Okay, see you later," he said.

The boys decided to get on the train that circled all of Disneyland. Exiting at TommorowLand, they bee-lined to the Matterhorn, which was their favorite ride. After a short wait they were sitting in a bobsled that was slowly ascending. The sound of the clanking gears, pulling them up, created a sense of intense anticipation. The bobsled reached the top and hesitated. Briefly, they could see a panoramic view of Disneyland below. Then, after a tiny turn, they were off. Screaming between gasps of air and thoroughly enjoying the moment, they careened down the rollercoaster ride ending in a blast of water at the bottom.

The remainder of the morning flew by. The trio had favorite rides and got to them as fast as possible. As the morning progressed, the temperature and the crowds increased. The boys stopped rushing, now that long lines were forming at many rides. Also, they were all starting to get hungry. They were in Fantasyland near the carousel.

"Dudes, I guess we better head over to the riverboat. Man, I hope mom wants to eat. My stomach is yelling for food," said Greg.

They strolled through the crowds toward the Riverboat ride entrance. Brett saw Mrs. Stephens.

He pointed and said "She's over there."

Mrs. Stephens was standing next to a long line near the water. She waved when she saw the teenagers.

"You boys follow me. I'm very impressed that you made it on time. It wouldn't be because you are hungry, would it?" she smiled.

"Yeah mom, we're hungry," said Bobby. "Are we going to eat?"

"You'll know soon enough. Let's go," said Mrs. Stephens

~~~

The group stood in front of the Blue Bayou restaurant. Brett noticed a gray doorway off to the side. *That looks sorta fancy*, he thought. *I wonder what that number 33 is there for.* If they had not stopped so close to the non-descript door, it would have been easy to miss it. Although Brett had been to Disneyland many times, he could not remember ever going through that door. Mrs. Stephens pushed a button and spoke.

"Hello, this is Jennifer Stephens. Could you let us in, please?"

There was a muffled click and the door opened. Upon entering the three boys stood frozen. To Brett it was as if the bright, colorful, childlike amusement park outside no longer existed. It was replaced by something vastly different: an elegant, refined, quiet, environment that oozed sophistication. They stood in a foyer facing an old style elevator and stairs leading to the floor above. Rich, dark wood surrounded them, creating a buffer from the world outside, which now seemed so far away. After taking the elevator up to the floor about, they entered the dining area. Brett noticed a few things immediately. Most of the patrons were very well dressed. The men wore expensive suits and the women, designer clothes. Also, though Brett did not know what they were, he noticed original framed animation cels, from Disney movies, hanging on the walls. After they were seated at a table with one extra chair, Mrs. Stephens smiled.

"This is Club 33. I told you it would be a surprise," she said.

"Wow Mom. You sure were right. This is classy," said Greg

"This is a five star restaurant and it is a members-only club."

Five stars must be good. If the food is as good as the rest of this place, I know I am going to like it, thought Brett. Greg Stephens looked up and grinned.

"Hey, look who's here. Hi Dad," he said.

A tall, distinguished looking man pulled out the extra chair with a flourish and sat. He wore a dark blue suit and hints of gray specks ran through his charcoal hair. Brett now noticed how much younger Mrs. Stephens was than Mr. Stephens.

"So, how is everything?" asked Mr. Stephens.

"Wow, this is awesome, Dad! It's really fancy," said Bobby.

"A business associate of mine got us in. I bet you never experienced Disneyland like this," said Mr. Stephens.

Brett noticed a man, with an alcoholic drink, putting a cigarette to his mouth. Before he could light it, a waitress had a lighter out at the ready. It was such a smooth action that Brett wondered how it had happened. He now also noticed that there were, at least, two servers at, or hovering near their table at all times. *Man, this sure isn't like the Disneyland I know. And, this service is unbelievable. It's like they know what we want before we do.* After they ordered and their sumptuous meals arrived, Mr. Stephens turned his attention to the three teenagers.

"So, boys, how is the summer going?"

"No sun and no surf yet, Dad," said Greg.

"How about you Brett? Are you having any fun?" said the kind man.

"Well the airplane trip was good. And, this is great. I've never been to a place at Disneyland this nice and where they can drink," said Brett.

"Well, we are happy to have you Brett. I think it is kind of special for all of us. Bobby told me you guys had a little bit of a scare on the flight to Catalina," said Mr. Stephens.

"Oh yeah, I forgot about that. My stomach was in my throat on that stall thing he did," said Brett

For the first time in Brett's short life, he realized that he was experiencing something that was unique, a cut above. Most of all, he recognized that it was the people he was with and their kindness to him that mattered the most.

After they had eaten, Mr. Stephens had to go back to work leaving Mrs. Stephens and the boys.

"You kids better get back out there. I want to leave by six o'clock. I'll meet you at the front of Main St. then," said Mrs. Stephens.

"Okay Mom. We better get going," said Greg.

"Thanks again Mrs. Stephens. This was great," said Brett.

"You are quite welcome, Brett."

~~~

As the three boys exited Club 33, two girls sat on a bench on the other side of Disneyland. One was smiling and doing most of the talking. The other's bright, blue eyes were looking to the sky in disbelief.

"I knew this was a bad idea. We haven't even seen them and I don't know if I want to," said Janey Jones.

"Come on Janey. Where's your spirit of adventure? We'll bump into them by accident, soon," laughed Stacy Small.

"Stacy, I don't like tricking guys like this. And, I don't even know what they are like. How did I let you talk me into this?" moaned Jane.

"Just because I knew they would be here doesn't mean it's a trick. Besides, these guys live at the beach. They are in the middle of everything that's going on. And, they are really cute, too."

"As long as we are just going to talk a little."

"Janey, you know I would never want to do anything but talk," said Stacy with a sly smile.

Janey was full of nervous energy. She was not adjusting well to her cousin's idea of a social ambush. *I just moved here. I don't need to deal with guys too*, she thought.

Janey stood up and started walking.

"Let's get moving. We probably won't bump into them anyway. I know you think if we stay in one spot they will show up, but I'm ready to go on some rides or in some shops," said Janey.

Stacy sighed, nodded her head and followed after her cousin. Janey, who was convinced that they would not find the boys, was relieved and started to enjoy herself. They explored Disneyland and forgot about their original goal. After exploring for the remainder of the afternoon, they meandered up Main Street looking in shops. Neither girl was thinking about Greg, Bobby or Brett. The girls walked out of a candy store. Janey carried a huge orange and white lollipop. Stacy put her hand on Janey's shoulder, stopping her from moving forward.

"There they are," she whispered.

Janey looked and saw three boys heading toward the main gate. A slight feeling of nausea came over her and she started to shake a bit. Stacy pulled her forward, with some difficulty, toward the unsuspecting trio.

"Hey Greg, Brett. Wait," she yelled.

Greg turned, recognized Stacy and smiled. Brett remembered Stacy from history class and cringed slightly. *Man, the social butterfly is here. I wonder if this is on purpose or what.*

"Stacy, what are you dudettes doing here? And who is your friend?" asked Greg.

"Oh, this is my cousin Janey. She just moved here from the valley."

"Hi Janey. I'm Greg Stephens, this is my brother Bobby and this tall guy here is Brett Sloan," said Greg.

Brett looked at Stacy with a hint of suspicion and quickly turned to Jane. He smiled when he saw that the pretty, athletic girl facing him seemed shy and a little nervous. *Hmmm, at least she doesn't seem like*

Stacy. When their eyes met Brett was dumbfounded. He felt an instant, invisible connection forming between them. Loving and lustful images came into his mind replacing his usual, logical thought patterns.

"Uh, hi Janey. Nice to meet you. Too bad we are about to leave," said Brett.

Janey was wringing her hands and wondering why her tongue and mouth didn't seem to be working. She felt like an energy field, thick with emotion, was surrounding her and this handsome young man. Janey involuntarily moved closer to Brett as if a hidden magnet was at work. Finally, she was able to mumble a few words.

"Er, uh, hi. Nice to meet you. "

Janey was close enough to touch Brett. Brett's face reddened slightly and he started to sweat. Now, it was his turn to be tongue-tied. This girl, who at first had appeared shy, was almost touching him and staring into his eyes. The feelings of lust were becoming more prominent. After a few moments Brett backed up a few steps and tried to gain control of his emotions and body.

"So you just moved here? That must be hard, leaving your friends and everything?" asked Brett

Janey relaxed even more. Her dreamy eyes stared into Brett's. She had the sense that she was falling into a pleasant whirlpool. Everything disappeared as she and Brett entered into their own special world.

"Uh, yeah, I guess so," she said.

Greg looked at the two rapt teenagers and smiled.

"I hate to say this, but we have to leave. It's too bad. We could have hung out. Maybe we can do this another time," he said with true regret.

"Oh no. That's really too bad," said Stacy.

Brett and Janey were still in their own world. Greg looked at Stacy. Stacy grabbed Janey by the arm and gently pulled her away.

"There's my mom. Hopefully, we'll see you around. Later," said Greg.

As the boys walked away, Greg turned to Brett and put his arm on his shoulder.

"Dude, it looked to me like you had something going on there with Stacy's cousin."

Brett was feeling the effects of the encounter and was a bit disoriented.

"It was really different. I'll say that. She doesn't seem to be like Stacy," said Brett.

"Well, she sure seemed to like you," smiled Greg.

Janey stared at the boys as they walked away. Her body tingled all over. Stacy looked at her and smiled.

"Welcome to Gundo Town, cousin. Maybe you will want to stick around, now."

Jane's dreamy eyes gazed far away, to a place that only she could see.

Chapter 8

Brett stood over his bed packing a suitcase. His mother called from the living room.

"Honey, are you ready? Do you need any help."

"I'm almost done packing, Mom. Five more minutes."

"I hope you don't mind that Kevin is driving. Your dad's car is in the shop."

"At least I'll get there," Brett replied.

Brett had mixed feelings about visiting his father. Since the divorce his relationship with his dad had not so much deteriorated as dissipated. He rarely saw him and when he did they didn't seem to connect. Brett thought about the sweltering summer days in Palm Springs and gritted his teeth. Even for Brett, who liked hot weather, it was not pleasant. Now that they were about to leave, the idea of Kevin driving with his mother by his side, brought feelings of resentment. *Isn't this dating thing going a little too fast? I can't believe she is with this guy at all. He's a total wimp.* The fact that his mother seemed happy did not help his attitude. Brett's stream of thought was interrupted.

"Honey, he's here. Let's go," said Ann.

After getting situated in Kevin's comfortable new, Chevrolet Impala, they left. Brett sank into the plush upholstery bracing for a long ride. As he thought about his mother's new boyfriend, he remembered the Disneyland trip and Janey Jones. *Man, I still don't know what happened with Stacy's cousin. I still can't stop thinking about her. I better watch out or I'll end up with a girlfriend.*

"Mom, how long will it take to get there?" asked Brett.

"It will take about two and half hours," said Kevin.

Brett thought about making a snide remark to Kevin but stopped. It was a long trip, and he did not want his mother upset for over two hours. Lately, he had snubbed Kevin's attempts at being friendly. In

Brett's mind Kevin remained a nuisance and an obstacle between him and his mother. The longer Ann went out with Kevin, the closer Brett felt to losing the life he was accustomed to. He knew logically that this was a normal thing to happen to his mother but, beneath it all, he was harboring ill will. Also, he disliked the idea that Kevin the dork might be telling him what to do some day. *I guess I better lighten up. If Mom likes this guy I should be happy for her. But I'll never let this guy act like he's my dad.*

As they drove, Brett noticed how few miles they traveled before the terrain was hot and arid. *I wish I was floating around in the waves at El Porto. This desert crap is not for me.* Thankfully, for the passengers, Kevin's car had air-conditioning. With nothing to do and not in the mood to talk to the adults, Brett looked out the window and daydreamed. He thought about being away from his friends and the beach. He envisioned pretty, sexy girls scantily dressed. Most of all he thought about another visit with his father, who seemed so far away in so many ways.

After an uneventful trip, they arrived at Derek Sloan's studio apartment situated near a golf course. Brett's dad came out to the car that remained running. He was shorter than Brett by about four inches and had the look of someone who spent time outdoors. Although he was only in his late thirties, his skin was brown and wrinkled from the sun. He wore shorts, flip-flops and a faded purple T-shirt. His eyes were hidden by dark sunglasses.

Brett was feeling a little claustrophobic after the trip. He pushed the door open with anticipation. He was overwhelmed by a wall of heat. After the comfort of the air-conditioned car, the stifling air took his breath away stopping him in his tracks. Kevin opened the trunk of the car and Brett's father took his suitcase.

"Hey kid. Let's get you out of this heat. It's a hundred and ten," said his father.

Brett walked to the window of the car and gave his mother a hug.

"Honey, you watch out in this heat. It seems worse than usual. We'll pick you up on Friday," said Ann.

"Okay Mom. I need to get inside. Bye," said Brett.

"See you later," said Kevin.

Brett turned and left without acknowledging Kevin.

Derek talked to Ann for a short time and followed Brett into the apartment.

Brett was soothed by the air conditioning after the short time in the sweltering heat. *Man, it's hot even for this place. I know dry heat is not supposed to not be as bad, but it doesn't matter when it's like this.*

The studio apartment was much smaller than Brett and his mother's. It seemed well organized considering how little room there was.

"Well Brett. It's good you're here. I have someone I want you to meet," said Derek.

"Man, is it hot out there or what? Who am I going to meet?"

"I have a new girlfriend. We've been dating for about a month now. I really like her."

Brett paused to absorb this new information. Now there seemed to be a trend in his life. It appeared that both of his parents were getting on with their lives and he would have to adjust. Adjusting was not something he wanted to do on summer vacation. *Crap, now, I have two of these boyfriend/girlfriend things to deal with.*

"Wow, first Mom starts seeing this dorky guy and now you have a girlfriend," said Brett.

"Yeah. Well, people get lonely. I guess you don't like Kevin, huh."

"I just know that things will never be the same. I think Mom deserves better."

"I don't know this guy but I suggest you give him a chance. You will be out of the house before you know it, anyway."

What his father said made a deep impact on the teenager. Being out of the house and grown up was not something that he had considered. *I'm starting to think about stuff I never had to before. Jeessh!*

"I am sure you will like my girlfriend. Her name is Susan. You'll meet her tonight."

"Okay," said Brett.

"And, I am really busy cleaning pools. So, I thought you could come along and help me?"

"Can I go in the pools after we clean them? It's like a furnace out there," asked Brett.

"Sure thing. We'll start early so we can stop in the middle of the day. Even I get wiped out when it's like this," said Derek

Brett looked around and saw that his dad had a nice color television. *I bet that couch is a hide-a-bed. It has to be with the size of this place.* After putting away his clothes, he plopped down on the couch with a Coke and turned on the TV. He wondered what he was going to do for fun in the five days he would be there. *I hope I'm not just going to clean pools and meet girlfriends.*

~~~

Later that evening Brett and his dad drove to Susan's apartment in a truck provided by his father's employer. They had dressed in slacks and shirts with real shoes for the date. It was still light and Brett noticed that there was a large swimming pool in the middle of the apartments. It had a slide and was full of people. Brett wished he was in that pool and not meeting his Dad's girlfriend. *It's so hot I'm not even hungry.* Derek knocked on her door. A short dark haired woman in her late thirties answered. Brett thought she was pretty but was still adjusting to the idea that his father and mother had significant others. After being introduced to Brett, Susan smiled warmly.

"Hi Brett. Your Dad and I have some fun activities planned for you. We don't want you to be bored while you are here," she said.

Brett was taken by Susan's friendliness and ease. She seemed to really care about what he wanted. He noticed that she too was dark tan and radiated fitness.

"Uh, thanks. Yeah, I was wondering what I was going to do besides help my Dad," said Brett

"Let's get going. We have a reservation," said Derek.

They drove to a large restaurant on the edge of town.. The name was Luigi's Italian Bistro. After a brief walk through the still sweltering heat, they were enveloped in a cool, plush, cozy atmosphere. *Wow, this is nice. I wonder how the food is*, thought Brett. As usual when meeting people, Brett said little. He listened to his father and Susan talking. After their food came, Susan turned to Brett.

"So, Brett, how has your summer gone so far?" she asked.

Brett was surprised at how direct she was and that he was the center of attention.

"Uh, er…okay I guess," he said after swallowing a piece of ravioli.

"I have a son who just started college. Are you thinking about that yet?"

"Uh, yeah. My Mom makes sure I don't forget. I'm even going to summer school for the first time.

"What about girls? Do you have a girlfriend?" she asked.

"Nope, no girlfriend. I sorta like my freedom," said Brett.

"Well, I am sure there are lots of girls who are interested. Tall and handsome is a good combination," said Susan.

Derek seemed to wake up as the conversation turned toward girls and dating.

"So, are you going on dates yet?" asked Derek.

"No dates yet. We saw some girls at Disneyland. One seemed to like me."

"Is she pretty?" asked Derek as Susan smiled with knowing eyes.

Brett was beginning to dislike the direction of the conversation.

"Uh, I guess so. I've only met her once. I think she's into sports."

They continued to talk. To Brett's surprise he liked Susan. He relaxed and felt welcome. *I see why Dad likes her. She's really pretty and nice.*

The next day Brett woke up in the air-conditioned front room and took a few minutes to remember where he was. He noticed the dry, antiseptic, cool air moving through the studio apartment. It reminded him of a motel room he had once stayed in. The bright, unrelenting morning sun streamed in through the sliding glass doors behind the hide-a-bed he was in. The aroma of coffee filled the room.

"Hey kid, good deal. You're awake. Let's eat something and get going." said Derek.

"Yeah, okay. What are we doing today?"

"Well, we have three pools to clean and then I thought we could go and do something fun."

"Okay, Dad."

Brett watched as his father went about cleaning a beautiful pool with a mermaid mosaic on the bottom. He wore only swimming trunks and flip-flops but was still hot. His father had refused to accept help but explained what he was doing as he worked.

"First, you watch for awhile then you can do some of the work."

Brett fought boredom as he tried to follow the steps that Derek was taking. He asked questions occasionally to keep his mind focused on the job but had difficulty caring.

"Brett, you don't need to just stand out in the sun. Jump in the pool. I'm going to," said Derek.

Derek dove into the pool and was followed by Brett. Both floated around in no hurry to get out. After Derek went back to work, Brett stayed sitting on the steps so that only his head was above the water. As always, Brett noticed how different swimming pool water was from the ocean. The chlorine smell, perfect clarity and warm temperature made the pool seem artificial and lifeless. Although the ocean was more challenging and at times dangerous, Brett felt that it contained life and energy.

By the time father and son got to the third and last pool of the day, Brett was helping with most of the cleaning. Although he made mistakes, a smile came to his father's face.

"You know Brett, you are doing okay," said Derek.

"Thanks Dad. It's sorta hard to learn in this heat but I'm trying. His Dad laughed.

"If you keep going like this I'll have to pay you. You could get rich working with the old man."

Brett laughed along.

"Sounds good to me, Dad."

They were almost finished working, when three teenage girls in bikinis laid down towels by the pool and started applying tanning lotion. Brett had difficulty keeping his eyes off of the slim, dark, bodies. The bikinis they wore were some of the smallest he'd ever seen. Brett turned back to his work while trying to keep his urges at bay. A beautiful, blonde girl gazed at Brett and then looked at Derek.

"Hi, Mr. Sloan. Who is your helper? He sorta looks like you," she asked.

"Oh, hi Gretchen. This is my son Brett. He's staying with me for a few days."

All of the girls looked up and glanced at Brett. He guessed that they were a few years older.

"Hi Brett. This is Hilda and Donna. I live here, at least some of the time. These are my friends."

Brett was staring with his mouth hanging open. Urges were beginning to make themselves known. *Man, these girls are super sexy.* Brett slipped back into the water.

"Uh hi. Nice to meet you," he said.

Gretchen glanced at her friends with a conspiratorial smile.

"Maybe we'll see you around town, Brett. We like seeing other kids here. It's pretty dead in the summer," said Gretchen.

"Uh, yeah. Maybe so," said Brett

"Well girls, it's time for us to get our gear and leave. It was nice talking to you," said Derek.

"Yeah, seeya later," said Brett.

"Bye," said the three girls at the same time.

In the truck, Derek smiled as Brett envisioned the three sexy girls in his head. Everything else was blocked out by his desire. *Man, lately it's like every girl I see turns me on, older women too. I have to watch out or I'll end up looking really stupid.* Brett snapped out of his erotic daydreaming and rolled down his window. *Oops, I forgot.* Even though they had been sitting in the air conditioned cab of the truck for a short time, the heat blast from outside was stifling.

"Why did you do that?" asked his Dad.

"Uh, I guess I spaced out," said Brett.

"Hmmm, I wonder why?"

It was early afternoon when they reached the apartment. After working in the heat and being in the warm pool water, his muscles were relaxed. The couch looked inviting as he sat down.

"Brett, eat a sandwich and then we can take a siesta. It should be nicer this evening. It's just too hot to do anything in the middle of the day," said Derek.

Derek, after not hearing an answer, looked around the corner to see that Brett was sound asleep though still sitting in an upright position. He grabbed a sheet and pillow, gently pushed Brett down and covered him.

The same routine was repeated over the next few days. Each day Brett learned more about cleaning pools and Derek found a fun activity for Brett when the work was done. Brett was gaining confidence. He felt proud that he was contributing and accomplishing something. On the evening of the third day Derek dropped off Brett at the local miniature golf course.

"Here's some money for helping me with the pools. I know it's not that much but it's something. Call me when you are done. Maybe you'll find somebody who wants to play golf with you," said Derek.

"It looks like they have pinball and other stuff too," said Brett.

"See ya later," said Derek.

Brett sat down on a bench. *Well, I guess I do this alone. Man, I miss my friends.* It was still over ninety and he was in no hurry to start a game of golf. The place was practically deserted. He saw a Coke machine, dropped in a quarter and grabbed the cold bottle. When he turned around he saw a teenage girl sitting on the bench. She wore a red tank-top T-shirt and extremely small shorts with sandals. He hesitated but was surprised when the girl waved to him. He walked over to see why this stranger was acting like she knew him. As he approached she grinned. Brett was taken by her dark tan, blond hair, bright green eyes and slim, curvaceous figure. He guessed that she was a few years older than he was.

"Hi Brett. Don't you remember me?"

She was so direct and friendly that Brett relaxed.

"Uh, er, uh, maybe?"

"How can you not remember?" she teased. "You were at my house just a few days ago,"

Then it dawned on Brett. Out of her bathing suit he had not recognized Gretchen from the other day. He was surprised that this sexy older girl would be talking with him.

"Oh, it's Gretchen, right?" asked Brett

"You did remember. Susan told me you didn't know anybody. So, I thought you might like some company. She said you were coming here.

"Oh, you know my Dad's girlfriend? I just met her but she seems nice."

"Yeah, I work with her some. We're buddies. She's really great."

Wow! This is radical. A beautiful, friendly, older babe to hang out with. And, she seems to like me.

"How about if we play some golf," asked Gretchen.

"Okay. Let's do it," said Brett.

As they putted orange golf balls through miniature windmills and mazes, Brett learned that Gretchen lived in Northern California but her family also had a house in Palm Springs. She was going to be a senior the coming school year. Brett forgot about the heat and his friends back home. He was drawn to her all-around beauty. He told her things that he had never told anyone.

"So you know how to surf?" asked Gretchen.

"Uh, yeah, I'm pretty good I guess," Brett answered.

"I ski but I have never surfed. I think it would be fun. Where I live the water is really cold."

"I can tell you about it if you want."

"That would be fun. Maybe, before you go back. By the way, when is that?" said Gretchen.

"Uh, Friday. So, uh, day after tomorrow," said Brett.

"Well that's not much time."

"Uh, yeah, I guess it isn't.

"I have to get going. Do you want a ride?"

"Uh sure. That would be great," said Brett.

As they drove the short distance to Derek's apartment, Brett could not ignore Gretchen's long smooth legs and other physical attributes. An inner battle between his fear of embarrassment and his physical urges was raging. But, he could not avert his eyes from this gorgeous girl. When they pulled up to Derek's apartment, Gretchen turned to Brett.

"I had a great time Brett. I think you're sweet," she said.

She leaned over and hugged him causing him to jump a little in surprise. After a few seconds he hugged back in spite of the response is induced.

"Uh, I had a great time too. Maybe we can do something before I have to go back," he said breathlessly.

Gretchen pulled back with a twinkle in her eyes and a slight smirk on her face.

"Okay, as long as we are just friends. I already have a boyfriend back home," she said.

Brett could not hide his disappointment but agreed. Gretchen leaned against his chest and gave him a quick kiss on his cheek.

"Goodbye, Brett. Be good."

Brett jumped out of the car. The urge to hold on to Gretchen and pull her close was overpowering. It took all of his will power to let her go.

"Bye," he said.

Man, that was close. I almost did something stupid.

On the ride home to El Porto, Brett's only regret was that he did not get a chance to see Gretchen again. Although she seemed out of reach, he could not help thinking about her.

Chapter 9

Stacy Small dialed and waited for an answer. Her eyes displayed a mischievous glint. A notepad was on the desk in front of her.

"Hello," said a woman's voice

"Oh hi, is Brett there?" asked Stacy.

"Brett, it's a girl on the telephone," called Ann.

Brett came into the kitchen, took the phone off the counter and sat down.

"Hi, who is this," he said.

"Hi Brett. This is Stacy. It was cool seeing you guys at Disneyland. I love it when stuff just happens by accident," said Stacy in a singsong syrupy voice.

Here we go again with the BS. Oh man. How do I get her off the phone?

Stacy continued before he could answer.

"I was at the beach but we didn't see you. Greg Stephens said he didn't know where you were. Are you okay?"

"Uh, yeah. I was at my Dad's in Palm Springs. It was nice to go there but I'm happy to be back."

"If Janey and I come down there, will you hang out with us? We need friends. And, you know all about the beach," pleaded Stacy.

"Oh is Janey going to come down to El Porto?" asked Brett.

"Funny you asked. Even though she is a really good volleyball player she's sorta shy about the beach thing. I think if she knows we could hang out with you and Greg that she would come for sure."

Brett thought about the Disneyland meeting which still affected him.

"Sure, you can hang out with us. Does she have a boyfriend?" asked Brett.

"Nope. She just needs to meet people now, being new. She had a boyfriend back in The Valley but it didn't work out," said Stacy.

"Okay then, we'll see you whenever. I am usually at 43rd street," said Brett.

"Thanks sooooo much. We'll see you soon. Bye," said Stacy.

After he hung up the phone, Brett wondered what he had just gotten himself into. He had strong feelings for this new girl and had no idea why. *She's pretty and friendly but I am thinking way too much about her. We only talked for a few minutes. What is going on with that?* He wondered if he could be close with Janey but not have her as a girlfriend. What Stacy said seemed so innocent, but he doubted with her, that anything was that way. *I hope I am not helping Stacy to mess with Jane's head or mine,* he thought.

Stacy sat at her bedroom desk smiling. "That should do it", she said aloud. The top page on the notepad was filled with notes. She checked off a few items.

"Now, I study my notes and make a plan" she said.

~~~

Janey was on the phone with her cousin. Her internal conversation contained more questions than answers. *Why does she want me to go to the beach so much? And, this scouting out gossip and boys. It's all too much, too soon. I just got here.*

"Janey, I talked to Brett the other day. I found out why he wasn't at the beach when I went," said Stacy.

"Oh, really?" said Jane.

"Yeah, he was at his Dad's in Palm Springs. He said that he would be at the beach from now on. He also asked if we wanted to hang out with him when we went to El Porto," said Stacy with not an ounce of guilt.

Janey was not able to hide her interest once she heard Brett's name.

"I never said I would go with you. Did he really say that?" asked Jane.

"Yeah and he asked about you. It sounded to me like he felt a real connection with you. He said he felt like he was your friend," said Stacy fudging the truth a little.

Janey was now on a rollercoaster ride of powerful emotions. She could still see flashing images of the friendly surfer at Disneyland, who had so thoroughly shaken up her world. She could not understand why she felt this way after one meeting. *I don't even want a boyfriend now,* she thought. It was not possible for her to control her desire. Janey somehow knew that Stacy was stretching the truth as far as it would go. But, still she dreamed of being next to Brett, on the beach. She was being pulled toward El Porto, in spite of her reservations, which were fading away like an overcast sky being burned off by the blazing sun.

After assessing Jane's mood, Stacy continued.

"Do you have a bikini yet? You need one."

"I told you, no bikini for me," said Janey in a low-pitched growl.

"Well, do you have anything? If we're going to the beach you have to have a bathing suit."

"Okay, let's go look at bathing suits. We can go to the mall in Westchester. It's not too crowded," said Janey.

Stacy smiled and checked off a few things on her notepad. *My plan is working. We'll be at the beach in no time at all,* she thought.

~~~

Stacy and Janey were arguing again. Janey had been trying on bathing suits for about an hour. She stood in front of her cousin just outside of the changing room wearing a dark green, nylon, one piece bathing suit. Janey looked as if she had just stepped on dog droppings. Stacy was scanning each inch of her cousin.

"It looks fine but I think you should try on a two-piece," said Stacy trying to avoid using the word bikini.

"Why should I try that on? I don't even need a top."

"You do too have a chest. It's fine. Everybody wears a two-piece now. It will be easier to play volleyball in the sand," pleaded Stacy.

Janey thought about what it would be like to kiss Brett Sloan on the lips while wearing one of her new bathing suits. Goosebumps erupted all over her body.

"Don't even talk about it anymore. If you think this is okay, I will get one in green and one in blue. I still don't know how I got talked into this beach thing," said Janey.

"All right. But with that trim, athletic body, you should show it off. I guess you win," said Stacy.

Now that she had a few bathing suits, Janey felt like she was committed to going to the beach. Once her cousin mentioned Brett to her, she knew it was inevitable that she would give in. With the decision made, her thoughts turned to beach volleyball, swimming in the surf and being with a certain young surfer. Although fear colored her emotions, she thought, *I'll see how it goes. At least I will see Brett again. Maybe Stacy is telling the truth for once and he does feel a connection with me.*

Stacy smiled as she walked out of the store with Jane. "This is going to be a fun summer," she said.

Chapter 10

Brett sat at the kitchen table listening to his mother. She had been talking for ten minutes straight, which was unusual for her. His attention was starting to wander. *Man, what's gotten into her. And, when is she going to stop talking about her boyfriend? It's like she is a different person since she went out with Mr. Dork.* When the subject of girls came up, Brett could not help thinking about Gretchen, the older, out-of-reach beauty and Janey, the shy, athletic girl who he would soon see at the beach.

"Brett, are you listening?" said Ann.

Brett watched his fantasy vision of two smiling girls in skimpy bikinis disappear.

"Uh yeah, Mom."

"Like I said before, you can't avoid girls forever. I can see that a lot of them are interested in my handsome son."

"I think girls are great but I don't know if I want a girlfriend."

"Why not? What's wrong with girlfriends?"

"Let's not talk about this Mom. It will be okay," said Brett with a tone of finality.

At that point the phone rang causing Brett to heave a sigh of relief. It was Greg who wanted to meet.

"Dude, let's hang out at the Tiki Hut and talk. And, my mom said you can come over for dinner," said Greg.

"Okay. I am ready to get out of the house, anyway," said Brett glancing at his mom.

After leaving as quickly as he could, Brett relaxed in the freedom of the open air. As he walked down Kelp St. he wondered, *what does he want to talk about? I hope it's something fun. I'm sick of chicks and boyfriends talk.*

~~~

To Brett it seemed like Greg was rambling on, talking about nothing. Just when he was going to interrupt, Greg changed the subject.

"So, let's talk about Janey," said Greg.

"What is there to talk about? I liked her but I hardly know her."

"Well, didn't Stacy call to set up a meeting with us and Janey at the beach?"

"Yeah, but it was just to hang out with someone who lives here. That's all," said Brett.

"You have a lot to learn about girls. They think different from us. I think Janey really, really likes you. Especially when you were so nice to her at Disneyland," said Greg

"Yeah, I felt something with her. It was like we already knew each other. But it was just one time."

"Well what about your rule about not having a girlfriend? Are you staying with that?"

"My mom says I can't avoid girls. And, they look better and better every day. I guess I will be more open and see what happens."

Greg smiled. "You must really like her?"

"I like her some and I like other girls too. I figure I can try out having a girlfriend and if I don't like it I can break up. I'll just have to have rules about it. I'm not going to be following some chick around with a ring in my nose."

Greg laughed and slapped his friend on the back.

"Dude, that whole girl thing can be sorta tricky. No way we ever figure them out," he said.

"Whatever. I'm just thinking about it anyway. That's all," said Brett a bit defensively.

But, as they walked toward Greg's house, Brett had a funny feeling that he had made a big decision, without even trying.

El Porto Summer

Chapter 11

The ringing of the phone woke Brett from a deep sleep. The old alarm clock next to his bed showed 5:25. *Crap, why is somebody calling me now? Heck, mom isn't even up,* The phone stopped ringing and started up again. Brett pulled himself up out of bed and went to the kitchen.

"Brett here. What the hell is so important?"

"Dude, you gotta see this," said an excited voice through the receiver.

Brett yawned trying to clear his head.

"See what, Greg."

"Just get your board and come down. This is awesome. And, don't take too long," said Greg Stephens.

"Okay, this better be good. I need some coffee though."

"Don't make coffee. Bobby and I already have it made. Just get your ass down here."

"I hope this isn't some false alarm," said Brett.

He heard his mother's door open.

"What's going on honey?" asked Ann.

"That was Greg. I guess the surfs up or something. He was pumped up, that's for sure. I'm going to get my board and go," said Brett.

"Be careful. You know I worry about you."

"Don't worry. After getting hit on the head that one time, I always go out with someone. Have a good day. I'll see you later."

The sun was coming up and it looked like the day would be clear. He walked down Kelp Street with his surfboard under his arm. He wore a gray sweatshirt over his swimming trunks. The only sound was his flip-flops slapping against the bottoms of his feet. He was starting to wake up as the cool air blew from behind him. *I could use some java to get me going,* he thought.

60

At the halfway point, of his walk, Brett stopped to look at the waves. He was optimistic, but had been disappointed so many times in the past, that he was still skeptical. What he saw took his breath away. The rate and loudness of his flip-flops increased, as he practically ran down the hill. He started to sweat. Lines of large waves were rolling toward the shore. Only a few surfers were in the water and many of the waves were empty. He now realized that the wind he felt was blowing off shore, from the land toward the sea. It caused the waves to retain their shape and in turn make them easy to ride. Elation came over him. *Wow, this could be the best surfing of my life. Thank you, Greg.*

Greg and Bobby were waiting in front of their house. Both were grinning from ear to ear. After giving Brett a cup of strong, hot coffee Greg said,

"This is it dude, perfection. And, hardly anybody is out there. Wax your board and leave your sweatshirt here. You can drink the coffee on the way."

In no time at all, the three teenagers were racing across the deserted beach toward the water. The top of the sand was a bit damp from the night before and it was dark and cool. A group of about five older teens stood near the water waxing their boards. As the trio ran by them, Greg turned in a circle with his surfboard under one arm and yelled.

"This is awesome. This is awesome."

A cheer went up from the group as Brett threw his surf board into the water and dove in next to it. There was a slight shock when he was surrounded by cool water. As always, immersing himself in the ocean brought a sense gratification. This was his true place, where he belonged. Everything else seemed foreign. Like a drug was influencing him, he slipped into a trancelike state. His senses became acute as his entire body relaxed.

When Brett surfaced to the roar of the surf, he had adjusted to the temperature change. After pulling himself up onto the long surfboard, he began to paddle furiously toward the rolling waves that were breaking in the distance. When he encountered whitewater, he either leaned back and allowed the nose of the board to slip over the top or rolled over and under with a tight hold. After about five minutes the three boys were sitting beyond the whitewater and looking at large swells of water coming at them. They were spread out to give each other room to maneuver and to position themselves for the optimum takeoff point.

Brett spotted a wave. He easily turned his surfboard toward the shore and started to paddle. He synchronized with the incoming swell and it began to move him forward, toward the shore so far away. One last stroke with both arms and Brett stood on the board with one swift motion. He was moving down the face of a large well-formed wave. As he moved toward the bottom, he adjusted his legs and bent his knees to place himself at the best balance point on the board. At the bottom of the wave he leaned, causing the surfboard to turn into the wave which was now a long, overhead, blue-green wall of water in front of him. His mind shut out everything but the task at hand as he maneuvered back up toward the top of the wave. He raced ahead with the wave crashing behind him in a cascade of whitewater. After bouncing off the top of the wall of water, Brett again was moving down. At the lowest point, Brett leaned as the wave was formed into the shape of a long pipe. He positioned the board about halfway up the powerful wall of water, and squatted with his back to the shore. He sped across the wave as it curled over his head enclosing him in a clear window of water. After what seemed like minutes but was only seconds, he came shooting out of the tube and up over what was left of the wave.

"Awesome wave," yelled Greg from outside the breakers.

Brett smiled. *Now I know what perfect surf is.*

~~~

Brett, Greg and Bobby stood next to a wooden lifeguard tower. After surfing for hours the three were tired and hungry. The late morning sun shone down on them. A painted, wooden ramp rose to a simple square box where the lifeguard sat watching the ocean and swimmers. Greg looked up and said,

"Hey lifeguard Bob. Do you have to put up the black ball?"

A lanky, tan man with dark sunglasses and red swimming trunks was raising a yellow flag with a black circle in the middle, up a short flagpole.

"You guys know the rules. I get the word and raise the flag. I can see the surf is pretty good still, but you'll have to go to the end of El Porto to surf," said Lifeguard Bob.

"Yeah we know. But, we don't have to like it. I've never seen the surf this good," said Brett.

"Maybe it will be good later today when I take the flag down. You know that too many tourists have been injured from boards. Before we had the black ball we were always patching people up," said Bob.

"I sure hope it's still good later. No way we're walking to the end of El Porto with our boards. We're way too tired," said Greg

"Take it easy guys. I have lifeguarding to do. See ya later.

The boys waved goodbye and headed up the beach toward The Strand. The sound of a loud horn rang through the air behind them calling any surfers left in the water to paddle in.

"Let's put our boards away. Brett, you can keep yours at our house if you want," said Greg.

"Wow, thanks. It's a long way up the hill to my house."

After stowing the surfboards and grabbing a snack the three boys walked up The Strand to their hangout at the bottom of 43rd street. A small café, The Tiki Hut was located there on The Strand. There were a few wooden benches in front facing the ocean. Already, the rich smell of fried food was emanating from the small café. Brett thought of a large cheeseburger, French fries and a chocolate shake. His mouth salivated. *Man that snack we ate wasn't enough. I hope we eat again soon,* he thought. Steps led down to the parking lot and then to the beach below. There were two volley ball courts near the wall of the parking lot. A large public restroom was nearby on the beach with a simple outdoor shower. Locals and tourists alike congregated at the bottom of 43rd St.. This was the center of the universe for the three teenagers during the summertime.

The boys passed the Tiki Hut and headed toward the beach. It was late morning and the beach was starting to fill up. Already the volleyball courts were being used. Colorful beach umbrellas were to be seen scattered around the sandy expanse.

Brett was getting hot already. He noticed the smell of suntan lotion and sounds of top ten hits from transistor radios as they walked across the warm sand toward the water. The three teenagers took their time while soaking in the first great day of summer. Brett looked forward to following his routine of going into the water and then lying in the hot sand until dry. He loved being with his friends and observing everything that happened on the beach. When he was too hot to bear it any longer Brett was back in the water.

After being in the sun for some time, Brett headed into the water again. The waves were now smaller and less formed than earlier. The wind was blowing toward the shore which made the waves choppy and poorly shaped. As he waded in the shallows, Brett surveyed the situation. There were many people in the water. Brett knew that most of them were inexperienced with the ocean and its dangerous undertows. He saw that Lifeguard Bob was already pulling someone out of the water who was having trouble. *Man, lifeguards sure earn their money on a day like this. Those tourists are really dumb. And, there's so many of them.*

After body surfing, being pushed toward shore by a wave, Brett headed back to the beach. He found Greg and Bobby who were lying in the sand with some other teenagers.

"Oh, here he is now. These guys were wondering where you were," said Greg.

"Well, here I am," said Brett.

A skinny white-skinned boy with short brown hair smiled at Brett."

"I told Kirk here about Disneyland and Janey. She sure looked like she wanted to get to know you better," teased Greg.

"She seemed sort of shy to me. I just didn't like that her cousin was tooling her around to sneak up on people," said Brett.

"Oh come on Brett. Don't you like her?" said Greg.

"Just drop it Greg," said Brett.

"Okay, dude, okay. You don't have to be so touchy about it," said Greg with a smile.

Brett remembered looking into Janey's eyes. Feelings of desire leapt into his mind, which made him feel uneasy. *I wonder if she really likes me that much. She sure is making me think a lot.* Brett's thoughts were interrupted by two bikini-clad women walking by. He could not stop staring, in spite of his attempts to do otherwise. As he looked at them he wondered what they would look like with the tiny bits of cloth removed. Feelings of guilt and embarrassment started to pull at his emotions. He looked at the sky and grabbed sand with both hands. *I better cool it before someone notices. I'm glad I'm lying down. It's like I lose control when I see a woman.* Greg took a long look at the two passing women. Then he looked directly at Brett and smiled.

"Dude, how ya doin over there?" he asked.

"Uh, er, uh….okay" said Brett.

Greg decided that one teasing session was enough this early in the summer. He left Brett to sort out his feelings.

After a while Brett headed to the volleyball courts. He lay down on the side of a court and watched a game. *Man, what a day. Great waves and sunshine. I sure am tired out though.* He was overcome by the exertions of the day and slipped into a sound, dreamless sleep. In what seemed like a few moments he was awakened by a gentle push. Brett spit sand out of his mouth and brushed it from his face. *Crap I must have fallen asleep.* Lifeguard Bob was looking down at him with a bit a grimace.

"Uh, hi there," said Brett sleepily.

"Brett, go home. You fried while you were sleeping. If you stay here any longer, you'll burn til you blister," said the kind man.

Brett moved to get up and his back and legs burned with pain.

"Oh, no. This is bad and I know it will be worse later. I better go. Thanks."

Brett slowly walked up the beach trying to avoid people. He knew that the searing would only increase as time went on. *Man, was that stupid and I'm going to pay. I better go home and see if Mom can put something on this. No way I sleep tonight.*

When Brett arrived at home Ann was mortified.

"Oh no honey, you look terrible. This is the worst burn you've ever had," said Ann.

"I know. It just happened. One minute I was awake and the next I was asleep," said Brett

"We have to get something on that. It's gotten worse since you got home too."

Ann took her time applying a white cream to Brett's back and legs. His front side was not burnt at all. He cringed every time his mother touched him. Even though he knew the cream would help, it would not be enough. Brett pulled away in pain.

"Brett, I know this hurts but we have to do it. Maybe by tomorrow it will be a little better. But, you have to stay home for awhile and recover."

He thought about the night ahead and became more depressed. The burning pain shot through his back and legs.

"I really blew it this time," he said.

"You need to take it easy, honey. You can't fit the whole summer into the first few days," said Ann.

"Yeah, I guess so," Brett replied.

Chapter 12

It was mid-morning on a Tuesday. Jimmy and Freddy were lurking in the crawl space of a three bedroom house about two blocks from The Strand.

Freddy was covered with dirty dust.

"Are they gone yet?" he asked.

"Yeah, I heard both cars leave. Let's wait a few more minutes before we break in," said Jimmy.

"Man, I wish Dusty was here. We always did stuff like this together. He knows how to sneak into houses," said Freddy.

"He was a stupid ass. It ain't my fault he was flipping me shit. I had to pop him. Forget it. He'll come crawling back soon," said Jimmy.

"Yeah but you spilt beer all over him. Nobody likes that," said Freddy.

Jimmy looked at Freddy like he was about to step over an invisible line.

"He deserved it, the little slimy, asshole," said Jimmy.

The two scruffy, criminals crawled out from under the house. Jimmy had already cased the place for the easiest and most secretive way in. Jimmy pushed open an unlocked window and pulled himself through knocking over a large lamp. Freddy, who was now afraid that someone heard, scrambled behind. He landed on the floor and ducked below the window sill.

"Do you think anybody heard us? That was fuckin' loud," whispered Freddy.

"Shut up and look for money and other shit. The sooner we get out of here the less chance of us getting caught. I'll go upstairs and you look down here," said Jimmy.

The two teenagers randomly ransacked the house, leaving a mess in their wake. They looked in drawers, closets and anywhere else that was easily accessible. Both carried nylon bags to hold whatever they found. They were becoming frustrated when unable to find any easy pickings. Jimmy walked into a child's bedroom and found a piggy bank which he cracked on the edge of a dresser. Change and bills fell out on the floor which he put in his bag. Next, he moved on to the master bedroom rifling through dresser drawers. Downstairs, after not finding anything, Freddy was looking in the refrigerator for something sweet. He found a half-eaten pie and grabbed it. After rummaging around he found a fork and started eating. As he ate, he looked out the window into the back yard for signs of movement. When he was almost done with the pie, he saw a flash of blue behind some bushes.

"Jimmy, I saw a blue thing out there. It has to be the cops," yelled Freddy nervously.

Jimmy came hopping down the stairs and into the kitchen.

"Let's get outta here. I don't want to get busted," said Jimmy.

They scrambled around the house like rats in a maze, looking for a safe exit. They could see two policemen outside. Both had guns in their hands. One was headed toward the front door and one was in the back yard heading toward the back door. Jimmy opened a side window and slithered out silently with Freddy right behind. They crawled on the side of the house toward the back yard which was not fenced in.

Jimmy who was flat on the ground poked his head around the corner of the house.

"Wait until the pig goes in the back door," he said.

Jimmy held his bony arm on Freddy's shoulder while they waited.

"He went in. We need to split up. I'll call you after I get home. If you get caught keep your mouth shut. Go," whispered Jimmy.

The young thieves scurried through the back yard and went in different directions. A voice from behind them was yelling.

"Stop, police, stop."

Jimmy and Freddy ignored the yells and were soon hidden by the neighborhood they knew so well. A few heads looked out windows at the disturbance and quickly pulled away. Jimmy stayed low as he ran by the side of houses and through back yards trying to avoid streets. He wanted to distance himself from his pursuers without being too obvious. The angular redhead feared that he had probably been seen by someone. When the police were snooping around, people became curious. After a few blocks of running, Jimmy, slipped under a house to rest and let things cool down. He doubted that the police would have followed this far without seeing him. *No way those slow pigs will keep running after me. I was too fast for them to see me,* he thought.

After sitting, listening and sweating for about fifteen minutes, Jimmy started to relax. The nylon bag which was attached to his belt was light but he pulled it off and opened it. Inside were a few five dollar bills, along with some ones and change. He pocketed the money and noticed one other item in the bag. It was a large broach encrusted with what looked like diamonds and rubies. He remembered pulling it out of a drawer in the master bedroom just before the police showed up. *Man, this might be worth something. I wonder how much I could get for it?*

When Jimmy felt that things had calmed down enough, he started for home. He exited the crawl space and dusted himself off, looking around for the police. During his leisurely walk home, he thought about how he would sell the broach. He decided to make some calls and see if any of the other criminals in El Porto could help him, for a cut of course. When he got to the apartment no one was there. He dialed a number and waited for an answer.

"Hello is Freddy there?" said Jimmy.

Freddy came on the line.

"Hi Jimmy."

"Is everything okay? Did they see you?" asked Jimmy wondering why Freddy was whispering.

"Yeah, but I am trying to lay low. I saw those guns and freaked out. I just ran," said Freddy.

"Did you get anything?"

"There was a pie that I ate in the fridge but that's all I got," Freddy replied.

There's no need for Freddy to know what I found, thought Jimmy. *The less he knows the better.*

"Yeah I didn't get much either, just a few dollars and some change from a piggy bank. Not enough shit worth getting busted for."

"I'm afraid of those cops. I'm staying here for a few days," said Freddy.

"Good, you do that. No phone calls either. I'll call you in a week or so."

"Okay, Jimmy. I'll talk to you later. Bye."

I bet Dusty's big brother knows some guys who can help me with the jewel thing. I sorta miss him anyways, thought Jimmy.

~~~

At about ten o'clock in the morning, it was already eighty degrees on a rare day that threatened to be in the nineties. Two plainclothes police officers stood at Jimmy Brook's front door. Inside, Jimmy was in his room smoking a cigarette, because his mother and her biker boyfriend Norm were in the front room. It had been two days since the break-in and Jimmy was aching to get out of the house. After calling everyone he could think of, he still could not find someone to buy the stolen broach. Earlier, he had almost gotten caught stealing cigarettes from Norm, but slipped into his room with a handful just in time.

A knock came on the door.

"Cora, who the fuck is that," said Norm.

"How should I know? Maybe one of Jimmy's friends," said Cora, in a high squeal.

"Come in, whoever you are," yelled Norm.

The door opened and two serious looking men stood waiting. The shorter one spoke.

"We're with the police department. Does Jimmy Brooks live here?" he asked.

Norm stood up knocking ashes from his red shirt, causing a small cloud to form in the air. Both of his big fists were clenched. He glared at the two men with eyes darting around the living room until he realized that there was no back door. After trying to gather his thoughts he attempted to put the police officers on the defensive.

"What the hell do you two want? Your kind are not welcome here. And, I don't see a warrant, so fuck off," growled Norm.

The taller man who was dressed in tan slacks and a light blue shirt, with his badge clipped to his belt, smiled.

"Well if it isn't Norm the Biker. Hi there Norm. Do you remember me? You know Ron Oakes. We had some fun together a while back. This could be our lucky day. We were looking for a small fish and look what we caught," said the man with a hint of sarcasm.

"What the hell do you mean, cop?" said Norm.

Both men entered the house causing Norm to back up a step.

"What I mean is that we don't need a warrant to take in a wanted felon. You know that jumping bail is a no-no, big boy.

Ron Oakes pulled out his handcuffs and smiled.

"You know the drill. Turn around and assume the position," he said.

Jimmy had his ear to the bedroom door listening, but staying as quiet as possible. After taking a few minutes to absorb what was happening, Cora stood up. She started pounding her fist on the detective's arm, screaming

"Leave him alone, pig," she yelled.

Ronald's partner grabbed her shoulders and pulled her away. He guided her back to the holey, overstuffed chair and gently pushed her down. She had little energy left to fight back and sat sobbing.

The three men were walking out the door with Norm, who looked like a caged animal. Ronald Oakes turned around.

"We'll come back to talk to Jimmy," he said.

Cora threw a half full beer bottle at the officers.

"I don't know any Jimmy," she yelled.

Jimmy, who had been listening in the bedroom, laughed out loud when the beer bottle bounced off the wall hitting a lamp. As soon as the door closed, he walked into the living room. He bee-lined toward a half-full pack of Marlboros on a cigarette-butt covered end table and snatched it up.

"Get away from that," yelled Cora.

"That asshole won't need them where he's going," said Jimmy.

Cora continued crying. Her makeup, which was already splotchy, resembled an amateur watercolor painting.

"I love him. He takes care of me."

"You stupid bitch! He was just using you like all the other assholes did," yelled Jimmy.

"They didn't even come for him. It was you they wanted. I wish they would have taken you. You're just a freeloader anyways" screamed Cora.

"Yeah, well I'm glad he was here, for once. Even though I didn't do anything, he saved my ass," crowed Jimmy.

"You are always guilty of something, you little fucker," screamed Cora.

El Porto Summer

Chapter 13

Brett was sleeping in. After two days and nights of excruciating pain from his sunburn, he was beginning to feel better. It was late in the morning. He was in no hurry to be anywhere after having his first night of continuous sleep. Flaky peeling skin reminded him of days and nights of torture. The fact that it was dark and overcast was a good reason for him to take his time. He turned over again and closed his eyes. As he was slipping back into dreamland, a loud knock came at the door. *Crap, who could that be. Do I need this?* Brett rolled out of bed and answered the door.

"Brett, where have you been? Dude, we missed you," asked Greg Stephens.

"Hey man. Come on in. I'll make some coffee."

Brett started some coffee and the two teenagers sat at the small kitchen table.

"Dude, we thought you died or something. You aren't mad about me saying stuff about Janey, are you?" asked Greg.

"I'm not mad. I got barbequed, man. Oh, it was bad. Really bad," said Brett.

"What?"

"Oh, I fell asleep on the beach and got burnt to a crisp."

Brett turned around and lifted his T-shirt displaying peeling flakes of skin.

"How are you now? We've got stuff to do."

"I guess I am okay now that I got some sleep? What do you want to do?"

"Some of my friends are in Junior Lifeguards. Bobby and I are interested but I want to check it out first. They're going to have some training at Manhattan Beach pier.

"I don't want to be Junior Lifeguard. All the wimps do that," said Brett.

"You don't need to sign up. I just want to ride bikes down to the pier and see what they are doing. Why do you think they're wimps?"

"Oh I don't know. I have seen those guys doing their stupid drills and stuff. I guess it's just not for me," answered Brett.

After talking some more and drinking strong coffee, Brett agreed to come along for the bike ride. In truth, he was ready to get out of the house after being cooped up for so long. Also, the fact that Greg came to his house to get him, made him realize how good it was to have friends.

Greg and Brett stood with their ten-speed bicycles in front of the Tiki Hut. It was still overcast but the sun was flashing beams of light through in a few spots. The Strand was not as packed as it usually was on a summer day.

"Let's get moving. We have an hour before they do this thing," said Greg.

"What thing?" asked Brett.

"You'll see. It will be fun," said Greg.

They set out riding north on The Strand at a slow pace. They casually avoided walkers and other bikers. For the first mile they did not speak but settled in to a rhythm. They pedaled past the central lifeguard headquarters. It was a two story concrete building that sat on the beach in front of The Strand. Numerous yellow trucks sat in the parking lot adjacent to the beach. The US flag flew alongside the black ball.

"I know some guys in school who are lifeguards in Huntington. Most of them are on the swim team. They can lifeguard at a lower age down there," said Greg.

Although Brett was confident about his skills and experience in the water, he thought it was a lot of responsibility for a high school kid.

"Wow, really?. They have a lot of stuff to deal with. They are sorta like beach police aren't they?" asked Brett.

"Yeah, but that's not the hard part. My friend Mike Smith told me a dead, bloated body popped up in front of his tower," said Greg

Brett stopped and leaned on the curb. His eyes were wide and his mouth was somewhat open.

"I know Mike a little. Didn't he freak out? I sure would have,"

"It took him a few days to recover. He was sure it wasn't his fault but still. Man, I hope they pay those guys big bucks," said Greg.

"I used to think lifeguarding was the perfect job. You just wear a swim suit and maybe a T-shirt. You're at the beach. And, you get to save people," said Brett.

"Well, it seems pretty good until you think about the dead bodies," said Greg

As they continued the sun broke through. Soon they arrived at the Manhattan pier. It rose high supported by barnacled pilings. Brett could see fishermen with poles surrounding a large circular building on the end. They cycled out onto the pier until they came to a group of teenage boys wearing yellow T-shirts and red swimming trunks. They were listening to a lifeguard that both of them recognized.

"Dude, that's Mike Doyle. He's one of the best guys in the water anywhere. I saw a movie of him surfing in Hawaii," said Greg

"Yeah, he pulled me out of the water once when I was a gremlin. But, what are they doing way out here?" asked Brett.

Greg smiled and patted his friend on the back.

"I was told they were going to jump off the pier."

Brett looked at Greg with suspicious eyes.

"You mean like in the saying 'Go jump off a pier.' No way. It's too far down," he said.

The boys listened as Mike Doyle talked to the group. Brett noticed that there was a lifeguard boat below, moving up and down with the ocean swells. *At least they have someone waiting down there*, he thought.

"Okay, so remember. The first rule is that you jump as far away from the pier as you can. And, you try to enter the water at an angle, staying as close to the surface as you can. Then get away from the pier," said Mike Doyle.

A skinny teenage boy, with no tan, stood first in line. Although it was not cold he shivered. The strong, tan, confident Mike Doyle looked at the frightened boy.

"We have a boat down there in case something happens. We don't normally let you guys do this exercise. If we see the slightest problem the whole thing will end."

Brett watched the first boy preparing to jump. He knew that it took real courage to be the first. Brett guessed the boy was about fourteen. Brett had no fear of the ocean or big, stormy surf but he thought about hitting the barnacles at the bottom of the pier and cringed. He turned to Greg and said,

"I can't believe they are really going to do this."

"Yeah, it's sorta extreme. I don't know if I want to sign up now, even if I could.

They both looked up to see the skinny boy jump. Brett's heart seemed to stop as the young boy floated through the air. While falling he tried to lean as he was instructed, but he leaned too much. He landed on his back with a splat. Both Greg and Brett held their breath. After a few moments the boy's head popped up out of the water allowing them to relax. Brett looked over at Mike Doyle. His hands were grasping the railing like the pier would topple over. His eyes were looking to the sky as if in prayer.

"Okay, who's next," he said.

Brett and Greg stuck around for a little while before heading back. As they rode, both thought about what they had just seen. The usually talkative Greg, was silent for the first half of their journey.

"Well I've changed my mind," said Brett.

"Uh, about what?" asked Greg.

"Junior Lifeguards aren't wimps. No way I'd ever do that jump off the pier deal. No possible way."

For the remainder of the ride home, Brett could only think of flying through the air from high above and hitting barnacles below. He hoped that his fear would go away soon.

Chapter 14

Stacy and Janey exited the sedan in the crowded parking lot below the end of 43rd street. It was late morning and the sun was shining bright. Janey wore a dark blue one piece bathing suit. Stacy wore a neon pink bikini that left little to the imagination. Janey seemed to be trying to hide in plain sight while her cousin made sure that she was visible to all. They carried oversized bags with an assortment of beach gear, including towels and a transistor radio. Janey used the gear as a shield from curious eyes. Stacy's mother looked at them from inside the car.

"I'll be here at four o'clock. Have a good time. Be sure to call, if you need me for anything. The Tiki Hut has a pay phone," she said.

As the girls walked down the steps toward the hot sand, Janey's stomach started to churn. She could not help comparing her small chest and white skin to the other girls and women on the beach. She just knew that every single person was looking at her and laughing. She wondered if it was too late to turn back when Stacy spoke.

"Hey, let's put our towels down about halfway to the water. We can see a lot from there."

Janey remembered one of the reasons she agreed to come to the beach in the first place. She loved volleyball and was curious about how it was played in the sand. She knew that beach volleyball was different from the indoor version of the game. In spite of her curiosity about the sport she loved, Janey felt like she was standing naked, for all to see and could not get away. She frowned.

"Okay, I guess. Whatever you want," Janey replied.

"Come on Janey. It's your first time. Give it a chance," said her cousin.

After getting situated with a good view of the volleyball courts, Janey lay on her towel taking everything in. She felt the hot sun pouring down. The smells of the sand, ocean and suntan lotion assailed her senses. Janey was watching a volleyball game when she saw a teenage girl walking toward them. The girl was thin, sensuous and extremely tan. Janey saw her and cringed. *This is all I need*, she thought.

"Hi Stacy. Can I sit with you guys," asked the girl.

"Oh, hi Monique. This is my cousin Janey Jones. Janey, this is Monique Dupree. Sure, you can sit with us," said Stacy.

"Hi Janey," said Monique.

Janey put up an invisible wall. Although she wanted to be sociable, this girl intimidated her.

"Uh hi," said Janey.

After deciding not to continue talking with Janey, Monique Dupree put her stuff next to Stacy and lay down. Stacy knew that this popular girl would be a treasure trove of information and started asking questions immediately. Janey listened through a filter of insecurity, saying nothing. Other than her obvious physical attributes, it became clear to Janey, that this girl was very popular and well known. When, Monique started telling Stacy about her latest bathing suit modeling work, Janey thought, *I need to get out of here. This is too much. Little miss perfect is driving me nuts.*

"I'm going in the water to cool off. I'll see you in a while," said Janey.

The two girls barely noticed as Janey walked away toward the water. By the time Janey passed the lifeguard tower her feet were so hot that she was started trotting. The water seemed more inviting with each step. The desire to cool off and get away from Monique Dupree was strong. Relief was instant as she waded into the small foamy waves. She took her time adjusting. Although she had been in swimming pools many times, this was different. She was surprised at how much she enjoyed being in the ocean. It seemed to have more life that chlorinated swimming pools. The fact that the surf was mild made it easier for her. After a time she dove under a small wave feeling the full impact of the surrounding water. The upper part of her hot body was instantly cooled. She felt rejuvenated and, to her surprise, comfortable. *I may start to like this. At least I can escape to the water when I want to. Nobody seems to notice what I look like when I'm in the ocean,* she thought.

After her swim, Janey walked up the beach toward Stacy and Monique. Her heart skipped more than one beat when she saw that Greg Stephens and Brett Sloan talking to them. Brett came into sharp focus as everything else blurred. Janey's thoughts turned to love. She envisioned Brett holding her hand as they walked up the beach near the water. Suddenly, she was overcome with fear and desire both rolled up into a spinning kinetic ball of emotion. *Oh no! Brett is there. I look like a white stick. What is he going to think? Does he really feel a connection with me? What if he doesn't like me?* When Janey arrived and greeted the group, the boys nodded and kept gawking at and talking to Monique Dupree. She was giving her full attention to them while gesturing with her hands and arms which drew attention to svelte, tan body.

"Oh, I hear you guys are some of the best at surfing," she cooed

"Ah, uh, er, I don't know if we are the best," said Brett.

"Yeah, we do it a lot but we still have a lot to learn," said Greg. Monique scanned their bodies.

"And, you really look like you are in great shape to ride the big waves," she said.

Janey's nervousness was now being replaced with angry jealousy. She watched as Brett became infatuated by praise and hypnotized by sexual attraction. To Janey, Brett now looked like a dumb robot with a fixation on Monique Dupree. *I am really starting to not like little miss perfect,* thought Janey. She lay down and tried to ignore the interchange taking place next to her. It was like trying to forget about a rhinoceros in a small room filled with fine china. *She's nothing more than a pretty tan face going after any boy she can get,* thought Janey.

After what seemed like hours to Janey, Monique left. Brett and Greg came over to her towel to talk. Greg seemed especially interested in Janey's reaction. Try as she might it was difficult for her to get out of her dark mood and carry on a civil conversation.

"Well, how is your first day at El Porto going?" asked Greg.

"Okay, I guess. I am white as a ghost though," Janey replied.

Brett sensed a bit of irritation from Janey, but had no idea why she was in a dark mood. He felt tenderness toward her and wanted to bring a smile to her face.

"You'll get a tan. Just keep coming to the beach. It takes awhile. But take it slow. I got really sunburned and was pink for a week," said Brett.

Greg and Stacy both saw Janey's face transform from a scowl to a smile. Knowing looks passed between them. At first, Brett seemed to miss the signs that were obvious to Greg and Stacy. After a few moments, Brett felt the change in her also, but was affected differently. It was as if a soothing, emotional bubble emanated from Janey into him. As he started to lose his emotional balance, he looked for an exit. Greg noticed that his friend looked awkward and nervous.

"It was good you came to the beach, Jane. I think the more you do, the more you will like it. It was good to see you here. I have to go now. I'll see you guys around," said Brett.

Janey's eyes had now become imbued with an inner light which made her face beam. She forgot about her fears and relaxed.

"Brett, you can call me Janey. I hope I see you soon. Bye," whispered Janey.

Brett walked toward the stairs below the parking lot. Janey's glowing eyes followed his every step, until he was out of sight. She lay down her head hoping that no one could see how emotional she had become. Stacy smiled at Greg who was deep in thought.

"Greg, now that I have you here, maybe we can talk about all the stuff that has been happening this summer. I am so into hearing about everything," said Stacy.

"Oh, sure. Let's talk," said Greg.

Stacy and Greg talked about what was going on in their overlapping social circles. Although Stacy led the conversation, Greg was able to keep up. He too was a social animal and wanted to know what was happening. By the end of their conversation, Greg had agreed to go out with Stacy. He wasn't sure whose idea it was. It had not sounded like a date when they were talking but Greg knew it was. *This girl is sneaky. Well, I guess she must like me. At least we have stuff to talk about.*

Janey's face lay on the cotton towel. Feelings of sadness and dread assailed her. *I miss him already. Why did he leave so soon? I guess I am coming back to the beach whether I want to or not.* Janey pushed her head into the plush beach towel hiding from prying eyes.

Chapter 15

The pleasant day was ending. After checking in at home, Brett was back on the beach. It was almost empty. Brett felt an inner peace as he watched the hazy sun moving toward the horizon. A confluence of elements, at sunset made it Brett's favorite time of day. The light was not as harsh. It was cooler and the beach was not as crowded. Although it was not the case on this day, the water of the sea usually smoothed out creating a glassy effect, reflecting the colors of the setting sun. Today, a stiff breeze was blowing in from the sea toward the steep streets above the beach. It was blasting the medium sized waves into mushy whitewater. The sun was still two hours away from setting. Brett walked briskly into the water, rinsing sand from his body. He quickly returned to the beach standing near the lifeguard tower. He looked up and said,

"Hi Lifeguard Bob."

"Hi Brett, how's it going?"

"I'm doin' fine. No way I can surf in this though," answered Brett.

The lifeguard lifted his dark sunglasses a moment and squinted down.

"Yeah. The wind has really picked up. It's blowing the waves all over the place."

"I'll probably go in anyway and mess around," said Brett.

"Well, use your experience to stay out of trouble. I can't always see everything."

The friendly lifeguard replaced his sunglasses and returned to watching the few swimmers remaining among the white-capped waves.

Brett stood near the lifeguard tower and watched the ocean. He saw numerous medium-sized waves rising up, then crashing, without form, and moving in different directions. Wave after wave broke on top of or into others, exploding into foamy spray. The conditions were inhospitable, but nothing that would challenge Brett. As he watched, Brett remembered a similar day with Lifeguard Bob about four years earlier.

~~~

Brett had been trying to surf but was not making progress. He was determined but inexperienced and young. After about an hour of frustration, attempting to stand on the old beat up surfboard that had been given to him, Brett gave up and headed toward the beach. The board was so unwieldy that simple maneuvers were difficult for the young boy. Since he had no one to show him, even the basics, Brett was left to learn on his own. As he walked up from the water, he saw a lifeguard waving to him. He set his heavy board on the sand and walked over.

"Hi, there. What's your name?" said the friendly lifeguard.

"I'm Brett Sloan. I'm glad you were the only one watching me out there. It was pretty bad," said Brett.

"Hi Brett. I'm Bob Kincaid. People call me Lifeguard Bob. I know a little bit about surfing. How about this? I'll tell you some things and you go back out and see if it helps. Okay?"

"Sure, I can't be any worse than I am now. Heck I might even learn something," said Brett.

After laying Brett's board down for demonstration purposes, Lifeguard Bob talked to Brett for about ten minutes. He addressed the main reasons why he had been having so much difficulty. Brett was motivated to learn and listened to every word. He recognized the validity of what the friendly man was telling him. As he started back toward the water to try again, Lifeguard Bob said,

"Remember to bend your knees and lean a little forward."

When Brett was near the waves, he stopped and sat on his surfboard. He did not have to ride a wave, to know that the advice he had received would help him to be successful. It was as if letters in a jumbled word had been re-arranged in the proper order. It all seemed very easy and obvious now. After envisioning himself doing as he had been instructed, Brett paddled into a small, fast moving wave. He laying flat on his board for a few seconds and then stood up with his legs wide apart, knees bent and leaning forward. It took him only a few seconds to gain his balance and therefore control of the surfboard. He rode the wave for only about fifteen yards, but he felt like the universe had shifted in his favor. That experience was a turning point in the boy's life. He had conquered the impossible and he had used his head. Also, the young boy's feelings about Lifeguard Bob and all lifeguards were solidified. To him, they represented everything that was good and decent in the world.

~~~

Brett smiled when he thought about that first wave long ago and the help he received from a stranger. He was overcome with a desire to return to the ocean. Just as Brett was thinking about returning to the water, four younger boys, he recognized from the neighborhood, ran past him into the waves. Brett noticed that one boy was shorter and lighter than the others. *I'll call him Shorty*, he thought. He guessed that the boy was probably twelve years old. Brett followed the boys out into the waves and bodysurfed near them as best he could, in the unruly conditions. The strong outgoing current, tugged at him as he waded, floated and swam in the sea. Although he was strong and experienced, Brett had to work hard to avoid being grabbed by the undertow and pulled toward the horizon where the sun was hovering. *Man, this is a little trickier than it looks*, he thought.

About an hour before sunset, the other boys headed toward shore. It was time to go home. Brett also started moving toward the beach but sensed that something was out of place. He breathed in deeply, relaxed, and focused. Soon, he realized three boys and not four were wading out of the water. *Where is the other short kid?* Brett looked left and right, then up to the sand, but still did not see Shorty. The outgoing undertow tugged at Brett's legs, making him increasingly uneasy. Brett allowed the current to pull him a little further out toward the setting sun and looked beyond the incoming waves. He soon saw what looked like a little buoy bobbing rhythmically out past the furthest swells, moving toward the horizon. *Is that Shorty way out there? I better find out.* Without hesitation, Brett dove, and stroked through the incoming surf. The wide, steady current pushed him seaward, which increased his concern. *If I'm being pulled like this then that little kid won't have a chance.* Soon, he saw that the bobbing object was indeed Shorty. He swam toward the boy, utilizing the current to pull him toward his goal, knowing he needed to conserve his energy for the work ahead.

Brett looked into the eyes of the young boy who was rapidly dog-paddling in place. The kid was tired and scared, but not defeated. Brett grabbed his arm firmly.

"Hi Kid, what's your name?"

"Tommy Burns," the boy replied through chattering teeth.

"Okay Tommy, I'm Brett. We need to get out of here. Will you do what I tell you?"

The boy nodded, and some of the fear left his eyes. "Sure," he said, "Whatever you say."

Brett knew the only way to escape a rip tide is to swim sideways, away from the undertow. Because the river of water moving toward the sea was only so wide, eventually they would escape the current could swim to shore.

"Tommy, I want you to grab my shoulders and hold on. If you can kick your legs, do it."

Tommy did as he was told, and Brett started swimming parallel to the shoreline with Tommy on his back, kicking as best he could. Brett used a breast stroke and rapidly kicked his legs to slowly move forward across the rip tide. The current was still pulling them out to sea as they swam. After numerous stops to rest, the two managed to escape the treacherous rip tide. Tommy dog paddled as Brett caught his breath and surveyed the situation. Brett was tired because of the energy he had expended. Although he was strong, having the boy on his back was more than he was accustomed to.

Looking back to the shore, Brett could see how far out they were. The lifeguard tower that seemed like a tiny toy, was about two hundred yards back up the beach from where they had started. He could not see or hear waves breaking because the surf was so far in front of them. *Now for the push to get back to shore,* thought Brett.

"How are you doing, kid? Can you swim?" asked Brett.

The small boy was tired but looked at Brett like he was a superhero.

"I think so," said Shorty

"We have to get to the beach. Swim next to me. If you get too tired, tell me," said Brett in a matter-of-fact way.

Tommy nodded his head rapidly.

"Thanks Brett."

Slowly, with one eye on Tommy, Brett started swimming toward the beach. He knew that they weren't out of trouble yet. *I can't push this little guy too hard or he'll run out of energy. I better go slow.*

As the two moved toward the shore, Brett would stop occasionally. When a large swell came, he would position Tommy so that a swell of water would help propel him forward with little effort. After what seemed like hours, the exhausted boys were able to stand in shallower water near breaking waves. Surprisingly, Tommy was able to catch a wave next to Brett and bodysurf it toward the beach. Brett did the same. About fifty yards from shore, Brett saw Lifeguard Bob swimming toward them. His red oblong lifebuoy was trailing behind him on a rope that was strapped around his shoulder..

Brett looked to the boy, smiled and said "Go with Lifeguard Bob. He will be here in a minute. You were really brave Tommy."

Tommy smiled, too tired to speak. The sun was almost completely below the horizon when Lifeguard Bob reached them and took Tommy under his arm. "You guys in one piece?" he asked.

"We're tired" Brett admitted, "but we're okay."

"You did good Brett, you did really good," said Lifeguard Bob.

Chapter 16

Stacy and Greg were sitting in the movie theatre watching "Beach Blanket Bingo". Greg laughed occasionally along with many of the other viewers. It seemed especially comical to him when scenes of surfing were projected onto the big screen. The movie was about half over and Stacy was interested more in watching the movie than talking. Greg guessed that this was something new for her. He wondered if she was usually the girl who talked non-stop during movies. Stacy leaned over to Greg.

"What are you laughing at?" she whispered.

"This is so stupid. The surfing is totally phony. I can't help it," said Greg.

People next to them nodded in agreement causing Greg to smile.

"I can see you are interested in this. I don't know why but I'll try to keep quiet," whispered Greg.

"I'm watching Annette," said Stacy.

After about fifteen minutes, Stacy leaned onto Greg's shoulder. Since this was a first date, he was a bit surprised but wasn't going to pull away. Even in the dark he could see how stunning she looked. Her hair was made up and her clothes were stylish. Most of all her perfume, which he guessed was expensive, had a hypnotic affect on him. It brought a sense of well-being to him through his nose. Although he knew this was just Stacy, she somehow seemed more sophisticated, older and sexier. He was finding the entire package she presented hard to resist.

The movie was over and they were sitting in Greg's Mom's car in the parking lot of the theatre. It was just getting dark.

"I guess you didn't like the movie?" asked Stacy.

"Oh, it was something to do, but the surfing part was nothing like it really is. Those guys weren't even wet. What a joke."

Stacy batted her eyelashes and smiled as she put her hand on Greg's arm.

"What should we do now? I'd love to talk since we didn't much in the movie," she hinted.

"We could go to the beach and park in the lot in front of my house. We could look at the end of the sunset and talk," said Greg with a smile.

Stacy leaned into Greg while tightening her grip on his arm. She whispered in his ear.

"That would be great."

As Greg and Stacy drove back to El Porto, the conversation turned to Stacy's cousin, Janey. Although Janey had been tightlipped about her crush on Brett, Stacy knew that she was in love with him. Stacy liked the idea of her cousin being with Brett. As Stacy thought about Janey and Brett, she became very comfortable nestled next to Greg. However, Greg was having difficulty carrying on a conversation with her, while driving and thinking about what would happen when they parked. Male fantasies flashed through his teenage mind with increasing frequency.

"I want the best for Janey. She gets hurt easily when she's in love. I think she really is in deep this time," said Stacy.

"Well, that may be too bad for Janey. I think he really likes her , but that girlfriend thing is not what he is into," said Greg.

"Why? I think they would be good together."

"He's told me that he doesn't like being tied down. He said that having a girlfriend was like being in prison," laughed Greg.

Stacy thought about what Greg had said. After contemplating different scenarios, she formulated a plan of action.

"Well, maybe we can help them to get to know each other even if Brett is afraid," said Stacy.

"How can we do that? I am not even sure that I want to do that."

"Let's go out together. We can do a double date but we won't call it that. Okay?"

89

"Uh, you mean trick them?"

"Well, I don't think it's a trick if they both have a good time. Oh Greg. I really need your help on this," pleaded Stacy.

"Okay, I'll talk to Brett about it," said Greg.

Stacy moved closer to Greg.

"Oh that's so sweet. I am liking you more and more Greg."

They pulled in to the El Porto beach parking lot in front of The Strand. Greg's house was about a block away. The sun was almost down and there were purple streaks filling the sky, creating an aura of natural ambiance. Greg was wondering if Stacy would move over toward the car door but she stayed next to him. She turned her head into Greg's neck and started to pepper it with tiny kisses. The smell of her hair and perfume mixed together was intoxicating causing him to let out an audible gasp.

"I really had a good time. I like being close with you, Greg? Do you want me to stop?" asked Stacy.

Greg was in no condition to stop anything.

"Uh, uh, no."

Stacy pulled him away from the steering wheel over toward her. She took his head in her hands, leaned back and continued to kiss him as he followed. He began to reciprocate and give attention to her closed, puckered lips. As they moved in unison into a more comfortable position, Stacy's hips involuntarily jerked toward him. He was now completely overcome with physical passion. Greg felt a strong urge to push his tongue between Stacy's lips and was rewarded when he attempted to French kiss her. She opened wide allowing him to play with her tongue. Steam was condensing on the inside of the windows of the car as they continued to kiss and situate themselves. Stacy was now slowly moving her hips into him.

'Oh baby. Oh, oh," she moaned.

Greg slipped his hand under her silk blouse trying to gain access to the clip on her bra. She put up no resistance but held him tighter. After unhooking the bra Greg looked at her heaving breasts underneath her silk blouse. Her lustful eyes were wide and slightly dilated. She turned around and whispered "The buttons are in the back."

Greg was able to remove the blouse in seconds. He stared at her breasts that were still slightly covered by her bra. He pulled down one cup to see a protruding, erect nipple. She pulled his head toward the nipple while pushing her breast forward. When Greg started to kiss one breast, Stacy's hips began rhythmically jerking.

"Oh my god! What am I doing? Oh my god!" she cried.

Stacy pushed Greg's head away and grabbed her bra and blouse. She started crying while trying to get dressed. Mascara and makeup were starting to run on different parts of her face. Greg groaned and pulled away to give her room. He looked out the window of the car into the darkness that now surrounded them. Stacy finished buttoning her blouse and pushed the door open. She jumped out startling Greg who was trying to recover his emotional and physical composure. He was now confused and frustrated about what had just happened. Stacy, who was still crying, slammed her hands on the roof of the car and leaned into it. Greg jumped out of the car and looked across at her with a mixture of apprehension and caring as she continued to sob and convulse.

"Uh, er. Are you okay? I didn't mean to make you feel bad," said Greg.

"Oh, I'll be okay. It wasn't your fault. I'm sorry. I just get carried away sometimes," she said.

"Do you want to go home?" asked Greg.

After what seemed like hours to Greg, the crying began to subside and Stacy got back into the car. Greg followed. She pulled the mirror over to see what her face looked like.

"I look terrible," she moaned.

Greg was relieved that he wasn't being blamed for anything.

"Hey, you see what you can do about that makeup and then I'll take you home. I guess it got a little hot for a first date, huh," said Greg.

Stacy smiled. Her eyes were still like glowing embers.

"Yes it did. Stop being so nice or I may jump on you. I need a little time to calm down. I want to make sure I don't start crying again."

"Take as long as you need," said Greg.

"You won't say anything about this, will you? I just get caught up in things, sometimes. I'm not a bad girl," pleaded Stacy.

Greg smiled and gave Stacy a friendly hug.

"We just had a date. That's all. And, I know about getting caught up in things too," said Greg.

"You mean it. Everything's okay?" asked Stacy.

"Everything's fine. Let's go out again," Greg replied.

"I'd like that. I'm ready to go home now."

The drive back to El Segundo was uneventful as both teenagers tried to let passionate emotions subside. Although the words spoken between them seemed to ease the situation, there remained a powerful, sexual undercurrent permeating the car. Greg parked in front of Stacy's house. She turned to him.

"Thanks again for being so nice," said Stacy.

"No big deal. I had a great time," said Greg.

Stacy moved to kiss Greg goodnight but somehow missed his cheek and landed squarely on his lips. Without knowing how or why she pushed her tongue inside Greg's mouth. He responded immediately with his tongue and other parts of his body. After a few seconds, Greg pulled away.

"You better go now before we get into it again," said Greg.

Stacy jumped out of the car and blew him a kiss. He could see a certain glint in her eyes that told him she left just in time.

Greg watched Stacy slowly walk to her front door while straightening her clothes. She turned around and waved. Her body posture indicated that she was thoroughly frustrated. Greg knew the feeling. *Dude, she had you goin', really goin'. I guess she felt bad because it was the first date. She is lucky I was able to hold back. Some guys can't,* thought Greg.

Stacy sat in her pink bedroom surrounded by teddy bears. *That was close. I better watch it. I still want him, even now,* she thought.

She flopped back onto her bed in defeat. *At least we're going out again. But, what will I do the next time?*

Chapter 17

It was late afternoon. Greg, Bobby and Brett were sitting in front of the Tiki Hut on The Strand. It was deserted. Not the slightest breeze was blowing and the ocean was calm. *Man, it's as flat as a swimming pool,* thought Brett. They were discussing their favorite subject, surfing and the lack of decent waves to ride.

"Dude, it's lake pacific out there. Screw this. It's been three days," whined Greg.

"Yeah, we need to figure out something else to do. This is making me crazy," said Brett.

Greg's little brother Bobby had the look of someone who had just had a light bulb flash on in his head.

"Hey guys. I know what we can do," said Bobby.

Greg turned to his younger brother with a mix of curiosity and skepticism. Frowning, he again looked at the flat sea in front of him. Brett, who seemed hopeful, waited in anticipation.

"So, spit it out Bobby," said Greg.

"I've never been there but I heard there is a giant sand dune next to Rosecrans Avenue. Maybe we could go there and mess around?" said Bobby.

"Wow Bobby. That might be the best idea you've ever had. I have a few boards we can use. What do you think Brett?" said Greg.

"It's sorta a long ways up there isn't it?" asked Brett.

"Don't worry about that. I can figure out how to get us there," said Greg.

"Anything is better than hoping for waves that never come," moaned Brett.

Greg grinned and patted his little brother on the back.

"Alright then, I'll check the surf in the morning. If it's the same as now, we'll go," said Greg.

The next day, the sun was out, but the surf was again non-existent. Brett looked out the open car window as they rode up Highland Avenue. toward Rosecrans Avenue. Greg's mother was behind the wheel. The boys were ready for a change after practically living at the beach for the first month of the summer. They all looked forward to doing something different.

"I'll pick you up in about two hours. Don't go anywhere else. " said Jennifer Stephens.

The boys walked up and away from the road over a small hill. They stood at the top of a long sand dune that ended at a residential street below. Brett noticed that it bordered a middle class neighborhood. *This is sorta weird being in the middle of all of these houses. I bet the kids that live there like it, though.* On this day the dune was deserted except for long pieces of cardboard in different spots. Brett was happy that the wind was not blowing. He did not like sand blowing on his face and in his eyes. The teenagers brought two long, thin wooden boards that seemed to Brett like oversized skis. They also had a round plastic aqua-blue snow disk.

Bobby surprised the others by running full speed down the dune kicking up sand. His legs sunk deep, making it difficult to run. After a little bit he fell and rolled, laughing with glee. Greg and Brett pulled out a bar of paraffin wax and applied it to the bottoms of the wooden boards. They positioned the boards and tried standing on them as if they were surfing but in the sand. Neither of them had much success. The boards either slipped out from under them or stuck, sending them tumbling down the hill. After a short time, the boys had fine sand covering their faces, hair and the rest of their bodies. It was the most irritating in their eyes and hair. However, it did not deter them from continuing to try different things and enjoying themselves. Skinny Bobby even picked up a piece of cardboard and tried to slide down the dune.

After some time, all of the boys had worked their way down the hill and were now slowly trudging up to the top again. As they neared the top, they noticed two figures. One was tall and other was much shorter.

"I wonder who that is?" said Bobby.

"We'll see soon enough," said Greg.

As they neared the top, Brett recognized the two figures. *This could be the end of a fun time*, he thought. It was Jimmy Brooks and Dusty who seemed like overgrown rats. They squinted in the sunlight making Brett wonder why they came out of the dark hole that he pictured them living in. Jimmy had the plastic disk in his hand when Brett and Greg arrived. He was looking at it as if it was his.

"Hi Jimmy. What's goin' on?" asked Greg.

"My buddy, Dusty and I are just hangin' out," scowled Jimmy.

"Yeah, we know Dusty," said Greg.

"We were just riding down the hill. Are you guys here to do that?" asked Brett.

Jimmy had no intention of telling the trio that this was the quickest route to the houses below. After making up with Dusty, he wanted to case some homes for future break-ins. He knew that Dusty was the best at sneaking into houses and had re-connected with him for that purpose. Although this was a little farther than they had ever gone, Jimmy liked the idea of not being close to home when doing break-ins. Once they got away it would be harder to find them and if they were seen they were less likely to be recognized.

Jimmy stood as straight as he could with his chest out but still looked like he was a leaning, disjointed tower of tinker toys.

"I thought all you wimps ever did was surfing," said Jimmy.

Crap, here it comes, thought Brett.

"Uh, we do other stuff, too," said Greg.

Jimmy looked at Brett who was frowning.

"Why aren't you sayin' nothin', surfer boy," said Jimmy.

Brett did not like Jimmy at all. In Brett's mind, Jimmy was a skinny, oversized, sewer rat who would always take advantage, if possible. He resented that Jimmy was treating him like just another little kid that he could push around. Also, he surveyed the situation and felt that if it came to a fight, three against two would be okay. He expected Dusty would be gone at the first sign of trouble. Brett had learned from experience that backing down from bullies didn't work out. *Bullies like Jimmy always come back and keep hassling you if you act scared.*

"I don't feel like talking, Jimmy. Are you going to stay here and go on the hill or what? Don't you have somewhere to be? And the slider is ours," said Brett.

Jimmy's face reddened and his lip curled into a snarl as he dropped the plastic disk. He clenched his fists as his bony, disjointed body tensed. Dusty, who was standing behind him, backed up a few steps. Jimmy looked at Brett, pushed his shoulder hard and pulled back to take a swing. Greg and Bobby turned white with teeth clenched. Jimmy started to speak but before he could, Brett swung with a short concise punch. His jab was true and connected with Jimmy's nose. Jimmy bent over in pain and grabbed his nose which was now bleeding. Brett, whose entire body was like a coiled spring, glared at Dusty who backed up a few more steps and then at Jimmy who was still crouching. Brett stood on the edge of the dune facing inward. All of a sudden, Jimmy growled and lunged at Brett. In one swift motion, Brett sidestepped, grabbed Jimmy by the shirt and kicked him in the side. Jimmy flew over the lip of the dune and down, still holding his nose. He rolled a few times and stood up. The blood on his face was encrusted with sand. After a glance up the hill he turned and walked toward the bottom. Dusty wasted no time in scurrying after his partner. As he ran, he tripped and rolled in the deep sand. Greg and Bobby were staring at Brett with surprise and little bit of awe. Neither had ever seen their friend like this.

"Dude, you didn't mess around. I thought we were all going to be getting into it," said Greg.

"Jimmy's a punk and a bully. He doesn't fight fair. Never trust guys like that. I saw him beat up a kid, half his age, once," said Brett.

"Well, he sure didn't get to you. Where did you learn to punch like that," said Greg.

Brett stared at his friends with a steely glint in his eyes.

"I got sick of being beat up by guys like Jimmy. I learned some tricks myself. If I'm going to get hurt, so is the other guy," said Brett.

Bobby, who had been ready to run, just stared at Brett like he was a brave warrior saving the innocent.

"Oh, there's my mom. Let's get outta here," said Greg.

~~~

Jimmy and Dusty were walking down the street at the bottom of the dune. Jimmy's T-shirt was covered with bloody streaks where he had wiped his nose. Now, Jimmy stopped and sat on the curb. He took his T-shirt off, held his head back and applied pressure.

"Man, what happened, Jimmy?" said Dusty.

"You saw what happened. He hit me when I was looking the other way. I didn't even do anything," yelled Jimmy.

Dusty started to say something but stopped before any words escaped his lips. After thinking for a moment he spoke.

"Are you okay? You must be hurt if you didn't get him back?" asked Dusty.

Dusty regretted asking the question. He sensed how mad Jimmy was. Bright red blood continued to ooze out of his nose.

"Shut the fuck up. Surfer boy will get what's coming to him. A shit storm is headed his way and he has no idea. He'll learn that he can't fuck with me," screamed Jimmy.

After a time the two boys walked around the neighborhood searching for easy houses to burgle. They were not disappointed in their search.

Chapter 18

Brett sat in the rec room of the Stephens' home drinking steaming coffee. It was mid-morning. Mrs. Stephens yelled up the stairs.

"Greg, get up you sleepyhead. I made coffee."

A few minutes later with coffee in hand Greg, who was still sleepy, sat facing his friend.

"Dude, it's usually me who is waking you up?" said Greg.

"Yeah, I was headed to the beach. I thought I'd surprise you. How long until you're ready?"

Greg smiled.

"Dude, let's talk first. Drink your coffee," said Greg.

"Okay. Talk about what?"

"Well, you know I went out with Stacy Small," said Greg.

Brett remembered all of the things he disliked about Stacy, but bit his tongue. He did not want to upset his friend.

"Oh yeah? How was it?"

"It went great. We really hit it off."

In spite of his best intentions, Brett's feelings about Stacy bubbled to the top and came out through his lips.

"Isn't she sorta nosy about stuff? It seems to me that if you told her anything, everybody would know it," asked Brett.

Greg now seemed a little defensive. Brett noticed and kicked himself inwardly.

"Oh she just likes people and wants to know what is going on. That's all," said Greg.

Brett was sensing that his friend was a little more enamored with Stacy than he expected, especially after one date.

"So, are you going to take her out again?"

"Uh, er, that's what I wanted to talk to you about. She wants to do a double date."

Brett stopped to absorb what his friend was saying now that he understood that Greg and Stacy were an item.

"With who?"

"I would be with Stacy and you would be with Janey. It will be fun. Not a big deal," said Greg.

Brett thought of Janey and what a date would be like. He remembered her intense stare.

"I thought Janey just wanted to be friends. You know I am not into girlfriends and all that crap," said Brett in spite of his desire to be with Janey again.

"Oh, it's nothing like that. It's just to mix it up a little. You know, keep it interesting. Listen, I really want Stacy to like me. It would really help me out if you did this," pleaded Greg.

"I don't have much money. How much would it be?" asked Brett.

"Oh, not that much. We'll just go to a movie and eat some fast food," said Greg. "And we don't need to get dressed up or anything. It will be casual."

Brett wondered what it would be like kissing Janey. Then he stopped himself. *She might not even want to kiss me. She might just want to talk.*

"Listen, I'll help you out this time but this doesn't mean it's going to keep happening or I want a girlfriend," warned Brett.

"Awesome Dude. And, if you need a loan, I can help you out. Let's shoot for a Saturday real soon. I owe you one."

"What happened on that date? Jeesh!"

"Oh, not that much. We just felt like we had a lot in common," answered Greg.

But, Greg's face was turning various shades of pink and red reflecting more beneath the surface. As they walked on The Strand toward 43rd St., Brett thought about this new development. In spite of his reservations, he was now envisioning himself and Janey doing things together. Lately, it was becoming hard for him to focus on anything else. *Maybe she's different. Maybe it won't be like the last time,* he thought.

~~~

Janey and Stacy were on the phone.

"Oh I forgot to ask you," said Stacy.

"Ask me what?" said Janey

"Greg and I want to go out with you and Brett."

"Oh, I don't know. A date?" asked Janey.

"It was Greg's idea. Brett is his best friend. It's not really a date. We can go out to eat or something. Brett's a nice guy isn't he?"

"Did Brett say he wanted to?" asked Janey.

"Greg said he asked him and he agreed right away."

"If Brett said yes, then I'll do it," said Janey.

Stacy was surprised that she didn't have to work very hard to get Janey to agree.

"Great. I'll tell Greg."

Janey was glad that her cousin was not sitting in front of her and was on the phone. Her heart fluttered like an overactive butterfly. She was a bit dizzy and knew her voice would tremble if she talked immediately.

"Wait a sec," she blurted out.

"Don't tell me you changed your mind," said Stacy.

After a supreme effort to rein in her emotions, Janey spoke.

"No, I didn't change my mind, but let's talk about what will happen," said Janey.

"The boys didn't want us to dress up or anything. And, I guess Brett is nervous about going on a real date," said Stacy.

"Good, I don't want to dress up either. And, I don't think this is a real date. Let's make it more of just hanging out," said Janey.

"This is great. Greg will be so happy. He really wanted this," said Stacy.

"Are you sure there isn't anything else you want to tell me about that date with Greg."

Stacy thought about what had happened on the date. Part of her was sorry that she had stopped what was about to happen and part of her knew that she had to do it. It was the first time she had felt passionate abandon with a boy. The overpowering urge to give in to that passion frightened and thrilled her. It was a feeling she could not forget. Both she and Greg had been very near the point of no return. Even now urges bubbled up in her mind and body.

"Oh no. I just really like him," she whispered.

"Alright, Stacy. If you want to tell me what really happened sometime, I'm all ears," said Janey.

Janey hung up the phone.

I wonder how far they went, she thought.

Chapter 19

Stacy was pleased that her plan for her cousin was progressing. Janey, who only a short time before, had an aversion to the beach, was now talking to her about going again. They sat in Janey's rather plain bedroom. Stacy exuded enthusiasm.

"So, let's go tomorrow. Maybe those guys will be there. I want to see Greg again," she said.

Janey remembered how tightlipped Stacy had been about the date. *This is my chance*, she thought.

"So, your date went good, then?"

Stacy's eyes lit up as she remembered the date.

"Yeah. I really like him. He's not like the other guys I've been with. He's more mature."

"Aren't you going to give me any more details about the date? Is that all I get?"

"I told you everything. We went to a movie, we talked and he took me home," said Stacy.

Janey looked at her cousin in disbelief. Although she didn't like to pry, she felt that Stacy was only telling her a small part of what happened. Whenever she mentioned Greg, Stacy looked like she had entered a distant dreamland. That dreamlike state was something that Janey had experience with. She remembered what it was like to awaken from that dream and cringed.

"Okay cousin. You stick to that story. Let's go to El Porto tomorrow then," said Janey.

"Great and maybe Brett will be there, too."

Janey looked at Stacy who could see that Brett was a sensitive subject.

"Whatever," said Janey

~~~

The two cousins had been lying on towels near the empty volleyball courts for about an hour. The hot sun was beating down on them. Both were frustrated and for the same reason. Neither Brett nor Greg had shown up yet. Stacy was thinking about how much she and Greg had in common. She was no longer thinking about what happened in the parking lot only yards away. She envisioned her and Greg interacting in the social arena at school and elsewhere. *He's perfect. We both like to be around people,* she thought.

Janey was wondering where Brett was. Her feelings were less organized and logical than Stacy's. Janey had an overwhelming sense that she would never see Brett again and that her life would never be complete. It was as if all of her emotions were funneled like a laser beam into wanting to be with him. Janey needed to do something to use up all of the nervous energy that was building inside her.

"I'm going in the water," she said.

Stacy knew that Janey was agitated because the boys had not shown up. She felt the same.

"Janey, where are those guys? I'm starting to get mad."

"Yeah, I thought they always came to the beach," Janey replied.

Janey stood straight and looked around. After not seeing anything, she frowned and trudged toward the water. Her mind was filled with various images of Brett and herself. Before she knew it water was lapping at her ankles bringing a soothing affect. Although this was only her second time in the ocean, she now felt like she and the sea were old friends. She dove under a wave with arms outstretched and eyes closed. The water that surrounded her gave her a feeling of connectedness to the earth. It was like a baptism both physical and emotional. Janey stayed in the water until she was less nervous and less focused on Brett. As she walked up the beach she became excited. Two people were standing next to Stacy. As she neared, she saw that it was Greg and his brother Bobby. They turned and looked at her.

"Hi Janey," said Greg with a smile.

Janey wondered why Brett wasn't there but did not want to show it.

"Hi," she said.

Stacy was standing shoulder to shoulder with Greg who seemed to be enjoying the closeness.

"I asked where Brett was but they don't know," said Stacy.

"Why would I care?" asked Janey.

Janey noticed that Greg seemed to be zeroed in on Stacy. It was if an invisible energy field was connecting them. Janey noticed that Greg was a little flushed even for a hot day.

"Hey, Janey, I heard you know how to play volleyball. Why don't we hit the ball around?" said Greg.

Janey surveyed the situation and decided that it might be good to get her mind off of the absence of Brett. She was frustrated that Greg and Stacy seemed very together while she was alone.

"Yeah, it looks like the court is free. If you have a ball, let's go for it," said Janey.

After borrowing a ball, Janey and Greg hit it back and forth. Bobby and Stacy watched. It was obvious to both, that Janey was an accomplished player. With each passing minute she became more confident and carefree. Greg was able to keep up and seemed to be enjoying himself also. Janey asked questions about the rules and differences from high school volleyball. Stacy was surprised at how little exertion Janey needed to play. Rather than tiring, she seemed to gain energy over time.

"Hey Greg," came a voice from the side of the court.

Greg stopped and looked.

"Dude, how is it going?" he asked.

Janey looked at the older teenager. He was thin and very tan with toned muscles. *I wonder what he wants*, she thought.

"Janey, this is Pete Moody. He lives in El Porto and goes to El Segundo High," said Greg.

"Nobody's around. How about a game? I've got a girl too," said Pete.

Janey was surprised by this new development. However, her competitive nature asserted itself. *I wonder how I will do? Maybe I can keep up?*

"I'm not that good," said Greg.

"No big deal. Look at it like a practice or something. Nobody cares anyway," said the friendly teenager

"What do you think Janey?" asked Greg.

Before she allowed herself to think about it, Janey blurted out, "Yeah, sure. It's like a practice anyway."

A slim, very tall girl named Bethany joined the three and they started playing. Greg and Janey were overmatched by two older, more experienced players. However, Janey was not embarrassed or discouraged. This was something she knew and loved. She was skilled and competitive. Volleyball allowed her to get outside of herself. Her fears faded away in the heat of competition.

"She's pretty good," said Bobby to Stacy.

"Yeah, she plays at school. But I didn't know she was so into it."

After one game, both Janey and Greg were hot, sandy and sweaty.

"Okay, that's enough, guys. I'm dead. It was fun though," said Greg.

As Greg and Janey walk toward the towels, Bethany approached Janey.

"Hi Janey. You're pretty good. Do you play on a team?"

"Oh, uh, yeah. I played on my high school freshman team last year. I don't know about this year. I'm new," said Janey.

"Well, Pete and I both play for El Segundo. Are you going there next year?"

"Yeah. I was going to try out."

"Let's get together sometime and talk about it. We need good players. I know Stacy has my number. She has everybody's number," said Bethany.

"That would be great. I really want to be on the team. I'll be sure to call to set something up," said Janey.

Janey headed toward the water to wash away the sweat and sand. She now was feeling like everything in the world was bright. The beach experience, that she had feared so much, gave her a healthy sense of fulfillment. She no longer cared about being seen in a bathing suit. The social awkwardness and feelings of being an outsider were fading away. She knew that after a few more times, she would be in synch with the beach life. Most of all she seemed to be a part of the new town she was living in and the school she would be attending.

As Janey left the water, she remembered the one thing that could destroy her feelings of happiness. *To Brett Sloan I'm probably just a skinny, new girl.* She wrestled with opposing emotions. She was elated about fitting in and new doors opening but still sad about not connecting with Brett. When she returned Stacy was alone.

Janey thought about how one day can change everything. She now felt like the pieces of her life were falling into place. There was only one last thing she had to deal with. *Maybe this date will be good. I have to do something or I will go nuts. Maybe it's time to stop being so shy*, she thought.

Chapter 20

The sun shone into the classroom through dingy windows, making specks of floating dust visible to the eleven students sitting at creaky wooden desks. Brett looked around and thought, *I wonder how many of these kids will be here when this thing ends?* He recognized most of the students and was not surprised to see them. He knew that many had either discipline or desire problems when it came to school. The wooden desks seemed ancient to Brett who wondered if they were there when the school was built. Unlike most modern furniture, the desks were still solid after years of use. When Brett tried to move his desk, he found that it was bolted to the floor. He yanked open the top to see if anything was inside. It was empty which is how Brett felt being away from the beach and the ocean. *I can't think of any place I would least like to be,* he thought. *Well, it's only two days a week. I guess I can handle that.*

This was the old part of El Segundo High school that had not been renovated yet. El Porto did not have a high school of its own, so Brett attended school here, a few miles inland from the beach town. Because the school bus did not run in the summer Brett took the public bus, which to him was one more hassle to deal with. He yawned and looked around the room at the other students. Most wore shorts and T-shirts with sandals or tennis shoes. A short, balding, be-speckled man wearing a suit stood at the front of the room. *I can't believe this guy is wearing a suit in this heat,* thought Brett. The teacher wrote on the blackboard in chalk while talking.

"Good morning. Welcome to summer school algebra. I am Mr. Potter and I will be your instructor."

He looked at the small group of students and smiled. Brett could not tell if the smile was sincere or not. *I know if I was teaching this class, I wouldn't be smiling.*

"Before we start, please remember that you can only miss two sessions and still pass this class. If you miss more than that you will fail," said Mr. Potter.

With that the class commenced. Luckily for Brett, he had already taken algebra. In spite of only earning a "D", he had listened and studied. Although he felt that he understood the material, his test results were very poor. So, he was familiar with what Mr. Potter was covering. Still, it was difficult for him to stay focused, for most of the two hours. When the class ended Brett was ready to go to the bus stop, but hated the idea of being bored while waiting.

Sitting next to him was a diminutive, pale, nerdy looking boy named Donald Head who wore thick glasses. He, unlike most of the summer school students, did not need to be there. He had demonstrated that, during class, by asking and answering questions that the rest of the students avoided or missed. This was yet another opportunity for him to obtain extra credit. Donald was a very good student but not especially comfortable in social settings. He desperately wanted to be cool. *Brett might be the coolest guy in Gundo High*, thought Donald. Donald looked at Brett and tried to be as cool as possible.

"Brett, how are the waves?" asked Donald.

For the first time Brett noticed Donald. *Why is this nerdy kid talking to me? Why is he even here?*

"Huh?" asked Brett

"Uh, the beach, the surf, you know," said Donald

"Oh, the beach is fine. I try not to think about it here. It would just make me want to be out in the water. That's not a good deal if I want to pass this class. I don't really care that much, but my mother does," said Brett

Donald looked hopeful. "I heard a rumor about you and Jimmy Brooks."

"Oh, that. I don't want to talk about it," Brett muttered.

Donald's spirits soared now that he was actually talking with Brett. He continued.

"Jimmy is telling people you ambushed him and that he will get you back," said Donald.

Brett, now irritated, growled.

"He's a liar and a bully. He started pushing me around and I popped him. I can handle that overgrown, bony puppet!"

"Gee, aren't you afraid of him? When he used to attend school, he would take my money all the time," asked Donald.

"He doesn't scare me! He bails out if someone stands up to him!" said Brett.

"Well, I guess you'll be heading back to the beach now?" said Donald.

"Yeah, after I go to the bus stop," whined Brett.

"Hey, I just got my license. I can give you a ride," offered Donald.

Without hesitation Brett agreed. The thought of waiting at the bus stop and then the slow ride home made his decision easy. He doubted that he and Donald had anything in common, but it didn't matter. A ride was a ride.

On the way to El Porto, Donald hoped that this could be an opportunity for some of Brett's coolness to rub off on him. Donald did not have a built-in sense of natural, social intuitiveness. To him the only way to attack a problem was to study it. *Maybe, if I can hang out with Brett and ask questions, I'll start to find out how he became so cool,* thought Donald.

Brett had no problem with social situations. He genuinely liked most people. Although he was not as outgoing as his friend Greg, he could sense the invisible flow of energy between people and usually avoided awkward situations. Also, due to his surfing ability and natural physical strength, people were drawn to him.

Donald was starting to become a bit confident. He did not want this new relationship to end.

"You know Brett. I think we can maybe work out a deal."

"What do you mean by deal?" asked Brett.

"Well, I want to learn about surfing and beach stuff and you need a ride to school and home. Maybe we can help each other out."

Brett could see what Donald's angle was now. *Oh, he wants to hang out with someone different from the nerd group.* Although Brett was not that excited about the idea of taking on the responsibility of Donald's social needs, he considered not having to waste time riding the bus.

"Also, I am really good at algebra. I can tutor you if you need it. None of my students have ever failed after I tutored them," said Donald.

Brett thought about Donald's offer. *I don't really want a nerd friend but I think I should listen to him. Mom won't like it if I mess this up.*

"How many people have you helped?" asked Brett.

"Oh, about twenty or so. But, in different subjects."

"And you'll pick me up and take me home?"

"Yeah, no problem," said Donald.

"You have a deal. I'll even get you out in the water on a board," said Brett.

"Wow, that's great."

"Oh, and one more thing. We need to do something about that name," said Brett.

"Huh, er, uh, what do you mean?"

"From now on, between us you are Donny. No more Donald. It reminds me of Donald Duck. Okay?"

"Whatever you say Brett," said Donny.

For the remainder of the ride Donny Head could not wipe the smile from his face. To him life had shifted into another gear. It was better than acing a difficult exam.

Chapter 21

It was the morning of the date with Greg, Stacy and Janey. Brett was nervous. *Why did I agree to this? Oh yeah, I sorta like Janey.* He was walking down Kelp St. toward the beach. *How can I be so uptight? And I'm walking toward the water. I always feel fine when I'm about to hit the beach..* Although he was not a fearful person, Brett avoided confrontation and situations that caused him to be pulled out of his comfort zone. Although he was attracted, sexually and otherwise, to a wide assortment of females, he somehow knew that if he had a girlfriend, his days of freedom would be over. Also, he didn't really understand girls and it seemed impossible to learn what went on inside their minds. *Crap, this date thing has me going all over the place. I really am starting to think about Janey and me together. This kind of thing is great for Greg and Stacy. But, Janey and me? I don't even know why we are going.*

When Brett arrived at the Stephens', Greg and Bobby were sitting in the kitchen eating. Mr. and Mrs. Stephens were there also.

"Dude, how's it going? You look a little distracted," asked Greg.

Bobby smiled and Mrs. Stephens looked at Brett with curiosity in her bright eyes. Mr. Stephens also seemed to perk up.

"Uh, okay I guess. Are we still going on this date thing?" asked Brett.

"Dude, dude. Don't bail out now. Stacy would hurt me," laughed Greg.

"Oh, I think you boys will have a great time. I have met both of the girls and I really like them," said Mrs. Stephens.

"I just think this is fine for you and Stacy but I'm not really a dater," said Brett.

"Hey Brett, give it a shot. You'll have to sooner or later." said Mr. Stephens with a smile.

"Come on Brett. This is just a getting-to-know-you thing. It's not a big deal. We'll just go eat somewhere and hang out."

"What about clothes? What do I need to wear?" asked Brett.

"Just Levi's and a shirt. That's all I'm wearing," smiled Greg.

Brett frowned and Mrs. Stephens put her arm around him with a motherly smile.

"Girls aren't that bad, Brett. Just go and try to enjoy yourself. I am sure that Janey will be great company," she said.

Brett cringed a little and then tried to smile without much success.

Damn it. It looks like there is no way for me to get out of this. Mrs. Stephens has probably talked to my mom about it too, thought Brett.

"Let's get outta here. I need to get into the water," said Brett.

"Yeah Dude. Let's get going. Maybe we'll see Stacy and Janey down there," said Greg.

~~~

Brett lolled around in the water trying to relax and forget about the evening to come. As he floated and occasionally ducked under a small wave, he still was not able to put the date out of his mind. He had no intention of even kissing Janey but expected that he would be fighting physical desire anyway. Lately, that was a constant part of his daily life. It seemed to Brett like certain body parts did not listen to his thoughts and followed their own agenda. He remembered Gretchen in Palm Springs and his frustration. *I'll probably just get frustrated on this date. I hope this doesn't turn out to be a big hassle.* In spite of his misgivings, he saw Janey as a sweet, innocent, attractive girl. *I hardly know her and I like her a lot anyway. Why is that?* He walked up the beach from the water to find Greg lying on the sand. It made him a little mad that Greg seemed so calm about the date.

"Hey man. What else do I need to know about tonight?"

"Dude, it's all okay. Stacy is driving. She just got her license. We'll pick you up at seven,"

"Why are we doing this again? Janey doesn't seem like a girl who goes on dates,"

"Stacy wants to get her out and doing things. The first thing was getting her to the beach. Now that she seems okay with that, it's time for a little more social interaction."

A vision of he and Janey kissing flashed across Brett's inner vision. His heart fluttered. *Crap this thing is happening in a few hours.*

"As long as it's just friends. I don't need a girlfriend," said Brett.

"Stacy said Janey had a boyfriend and it didn't work out. I don't think she is looking for a boyfriend," countered Greg.

Greg looked away to hide the smile on his tan face. He was anticipating his friend's reaction when he discovered that Janey liked him more than as just friends. Also, he didn't want to tip Brett off that this whole date was for Janey to be with Brett.

After a day at the beach, Brett was at home getting ready for the date.

"Honey, I heard you have a big date tonight. I bought you some new shirts," said Ann.

"Uh yeah. How did you hear about it?" asked Brett.

"Mrs. Stephens called. She said that the girls were nice and really pretty."

"I'm not much of a dating guy. I just want it over with," said Brett.

"Here, let me see how you look in these shirts."

"Okay but I don't know why this is such a big deal."

After modeling shirts for his mother, Brett wore the one that she liked. He was feeling that a huge wave was about to crash on top of him. Although he still wanted to convince himself that the date would not be a big event, he sensed that he might be wrong. A car horn honked from the street. He walked toward the door. Ann gave him a hug and said.

"You look really cute, honey. Have a good time.

"I'll try Mom," said Brett.

~~~

Brett looked at the four-door sedan and noticed that Stacy and Greg were in the front seat. Janey was in the back with the door open. A wave of delicate perfume hit Brett's senses as soon as he entered the car. He gasped slightly when he saw Janey. She was wearing makeup that had been applied with subtlety and her hair was styled. She wore smooth nylons under a short skirt. A beige, silk, low-cut blouse completed a stunning outfit. Brett was taken by the new Janey who now seemed more like a woman than a girl.

Brett paused with the realization that what he expected was not what was happening. *So, we aren't getting dressed up huh? Just casual, huh? I don't even recognize Janey. It's like she got the movie star treatment. What else is going to happen?* Janey turned toward Brett with a faraway look in her accented, mascara-lined eyes and said, "hi Brett. It's great to see you."

Brett could feel a warm glow emanating from Janey. Her eyes pierced his mind. It was as if they had entered another room, separate from the world. He felt close to her, but also uneasy. *Damn, who is this girl? Where did Janey disappear to?* Brett sat down but kept some distance between the new Janey and himself. He was extremely attracted to her but also flustered. *I need to get used to this. She is getting me turned on and it's only been a few minutes.*

"Hi Jane. You look really nice," said Brett.

Janey frowned a bit, biting her lipstick covered lip, allowing the old, recognizable Janey to emerge. Her expression was one of mock frustration.

"Brett, I thought we were friends. Please call me Janey," she said.

"Okay, I'll do that," said Brett stiffly.

Stacy and Greg turned around in the back seat.

"Dude, this is great. We are all here and ready to go," said Greg.

"Yeah, I guess this is it. The casual date," said Brett sarcastically.

"We never get to dress up, Brett. Don't mind us girls," said
Stacy. "Besides, we're celebrating me getting my license."

Brett was now feeling underdressed and underprepared.

"Whatever," he said

"We're going to drive around for awhile before we go to dinner.
I thought we could go to that new seafood place by the Manhattan
Pier," said Greg.

As they drove, Brett looked out the window trying to adjust. He
could not help being attracted to the new Janey. After a time he
noticed that Janey had retreated to her window and was looking out
of place and awkward. It made Brett think of meeting her at
Disneyland. He guessed that it was he and not Stacy who was most
likely the reason for her being upset. A tinge of guilt crept into his
irritated, nervous mind. *Crap, she wanted a nice time and I'm acting like a
dork*, he thought. *Hell, I'm here now. I might as well make the best of it. No
reason for all that makeup work to go to waste.*

"Hey Janey, I'm sorry. I guess I'm not used to this dating thing,"
said Brett.

She brightened immediately at hearing that she was not the only
person in the car who was ill at ease. She leaned toward Brett and
whispered, "I told Stacy this was too much. I never put on makeup
and dress up like this. She made me to do it."

Again Brett inhaled her perfume and saw how visually stunning
she looked. In spite of his determination to only be friends, he could
not help but be drawn to her. He moved toward her until they were
sitting next to each other.

"Well, I have to admit that you look really great," he said.

How did I end up this close, he thought? She smiled and he noticed
that faraway look in her eyes again. *I wonder what that look means? I
guess she needed me to be a little nicer.*

As they drove, they talked. Janey relaxed and opened up to Brett.
He, in turn, felt a connection with her that was foreign to him. It was
deeper than anything he had ever experienced. As each minute
passed they learned more about each other. To Janey, this was the

boyfriend of her dreams. He was strong, kind and handsome. He didn't always talk about himself but seemed genuinely interested in her feelings.

From the front seat Stacy asked "How are you two doing back there?"

She smiled when there was no answer. She had been observing by using the mirror when she could. It was obvious that her plan was working. *I guess that little bit of perfume and eyeliner did work*, she thought.

The seafood restaurant was nice but not too fancy or expensive. Stacy tried to initiate conversation. Greg and Janey responded with small talk about the summer. Brett was silent and focused on his food. Greg tried to get his friend to say something. When he had little success, he looked at Janey and smiled.

"Hey Janey. Did you know that Brett saved a kid the other day. He probably would have drowned," said Greg.

Brett turned a little red as Janey looked at him with admiration.

"Wow. That's amazing Brett," said Janey.

"Well, it isn't that big of a deal," Brett replied.

Greg wouldn't let that statement pass.

"Don't let him fool you. It is a big deal. I heard the kid was halfway to Catalina and Brett pulled him almost the whole way back to shore."

"Oh Brett I think that's fantastic. Please tell us more about the ocean and surfing," Janey pleaded.

Brett was now thinking about being in the water and felt at ease. He forgot to be self-conscious and opened up about the various water activities that he engaged in. Janey, who was more than impressed, asked questions. Greg added bits of interesting information about Brett to the conversation. By the end of dinner Janey felt closer to Brett than she ever had to anyone. To her his openness was an invitation for her romantic feelings to expand and gain momentum.

After dinner Stacy drove back toward El Porto to drop off Brett and Greg. Janey was sitting next to Brett in a comfortable way. She seemed to be waiting for something. This was the closest Brett had ever been to a girl for an extended amount of time. *What am I supposed to do now?* He started to situate himself to accommodate Janey. To his surprise she grabbed his arm and pulled it around and onto her shoulder. Then, she laid her head on his chest. He could almost hear her purring contentedly. This new level of intimacy also had a physical effect. He was becoming physically stimulated. *Crap, this always happens. God, I hope she doesn't notice.* They said nothing on the drive home. By the time they arrived at Brett's apartment, Brett felt like they were glued together. He started the ungluing process but Janey did not seem in a hurry to let go.

"Well, uh. We're here at my house," said Brett.

Janey looked up. He could see a slight glistening in her eyes. As he tried to figure out what was happening, Janey grabbed the back of his head and pulled it to her lips. She kissed him hard and would not let go. Brett was surprised but also embarrassed due to his strong physical reaction. He found himself returning her kisses and liking it very much. When her tongue wormed its way into his mouth Brett felt intense, sexual desire rise up like a huge ocean swell coming from the horizon. After what seemed like hours of sensuous kissing, Brett's hands started to move up and down Janey's back. He felt that if he was in that car for another minute he would try to do more and regret it. He remembered there were others with them and reined in his sexual urges. *Uh oh, I better get out of here before I rip that blouse off her.* Brett pulled away abruptly and jumped out of the car.

"Uh, I had a good time. I'll see you guys' around," he said.

As he walked away Brett could see Janey sobbing through the window of the car. Stacy scowled as she smashed her foot on the gas pedal, causing the wheels to screech up Kelp St.. Brett could not stop thinking about what Janey's tongue had done to his usually controlled state of mind. *I knew this was going to be trouble. Man, she had me ready to do things that I hadn't even thought of. Maybe Greg can explain to me what just happened.*

Chapter 22

It was another beautiful, sunny, summer day. Brett, who sat next to Donny Head in his parents' car, frowned when thinking about the summer school class that had just ended. As they drove to El Porto, Brett wished he was wading into the ocean and not worrying about algebra. *Man, I hope Donny can help me with this crap. I sure don't have a clue. I used to know this stuff and now I really don't care enough to concentrate.*

"So, today we start the tutoring?" asked Brett.

"Uh, do you have a bike? You know a ten speed or something?" asked Donny.

Brett was a little irritated at the change of subject but answered. "Yeah, I have a nice bike."

"Okay, we need to take a bike ride on The Strand. It will take about an hour. Then we can do some studying."

Brett was now wondering if working with Donny was a good idea. His goal was to get the schoolwork over with, say goodbye to Donny and go to the beach. This was starting to seem like too much time and too much work.

"I thought we were going to do the studying? Why the bike ride?" moaned Brett.

Brett expected Donny to back off like a timid nerd, but was surprised by his confidence.

"Just let me handle the tutoring part. You can handle the surfing stuff. Okay?"

"Oh, alright. Are you sure you never fail at this?" asked Brett. "Yup."

After parking the car in front of Brett's apartment, Donny opened the trunk. To Brett's surprise he pulled out a bright pink girl's bicycle with plastic ribbons hanging from the handle bars. Donny was dressed in dark slacks and a long-sleeved, plaid shirt that had pens and pencils in the pocket. Sweat was pouring from his red forehead down his face. Brett could not help but laugh out loud.

"Are you really going to ride that thing down The Strand? And, aren't you a little overdressed?"

"Uh, I was going to. This is my sister's bike. I don't have one," said Donny.

"Okay, but I will tell you what to wear next time. You won't be very comfortable wearing those clothes. I'd let you wear my stuff but I think you're too small. I'll see what I have."

~~~

Brett and Donny rode along The Strand at a leisurely pace. Donny was wearing one of Brett's old T-shirts but still had on the slacks. Smiling heads turned as they passed walkers and other cyclists. One young boy made a smartass remark as they passed. Brett tried to ignore it.

"So, here we are riding bikes. The question is why?" said Brett.

"Uh yeah, Brett. So this is the part where I tell you how we will make you perfect in algebra.

"Right now, I feel like I will never get it? I am having a hard time getting motivated," said Brett.

"Tell me about when you learned to surf. Did you have someone helping you? Was it easy?" asked Donny.

"No way. I did it myself. When I started it seemed like it took forever. It was really hard."

"So why do you think you were able to do it? I bet a lot of guys would just give up?" asked Donny.

Brett was still trying to figure out why they were on this ride and what the questions had to do with learning algebra.

"I decided that I would keep trying until I was good at it. Actually, I was a little pissed off about it," said Brett.

"To be good at something you need three things. The first is desire, the second is commitment and the third is some intelligence. Learning algebra is the same as learning surfing or anything else."

"I don't believe that. Surfing isn't the same as math," said Brett.

"The only reason you haven't done well, in your studies, is that you haven't decided to make the commitment. If you do that, I will show you how to do the studying. Mostly, it's repetition and having the right approach."

"I try at math but it isn't working. I think I have it and then I screw up the tests."

"Listen to me and think about a couple of things. If you worked as hard at math as you have at learning to surf, would it make a difference? Also, if you had a few good tips on surfing would it have taken less time to learn?" said Donny.

In spite of Brett's reservations, as they cycled back to his apartment, he began to see the simple logic of what Donny was telling him. He also realized that looking at Donny as an awkward nerd might limit his learning. *I better give this guy a chance if I want this to work*, thought Brett.

When they walked into the apartment, Ann looked up and could not help smiling at the skinny, red-faced boy with Brett.

"Hi honey. Who is your friend?" she asked.

"This is Donny Head. He's in my algebra class. We are going to study together," said Brett.

"Hi Donny. I like that Brett is studying. I have a feeling that you know how to study," said Ann.

"Uh, hi Mrs. Sloan. Yeah I've studied a lot," answered Donny.

"You boys go ahead. I will have dinner ready in an hour or so. "

"Okay, Mom.

Brett braced himself for a boring study session. He knew that this would be easy for Donny, even if it was painful for him. He did not like being the ignorant, awkward one. *I guess we might as well get it over with.*

To Brett's surprise the study session wasn't that difficult. Donny talked about what needed to be covered and what Brett needed to do to succeed. It was obvious that Donny had a plan and expected complete success. As the steps were shown to him, Brett became confident as well.

"If you follow the steps, you will get an A. You have an advantage now. You have time to study and you are only studying one thing," said Donny.

"So why do I take practice tests?" asked Brett.

"When you take a real test, it won't be much different from what you are already doing with the practice tests. Also, the more you go over this stuff, in different ways, the better you learn it," said Donny.

"Okay, Donny. I'll do what you say and see what happens," said Brett.

"Just do one step at a time. Like anything it will take awhile to get moving but once you do, it will be easy."

Brett thought back to those early failures when learning to surf and frowned. He knew that if he had followed a plan like Donny's, it would have been much easier. Brett smiled with the realization that he was wrong about his nerdy tutor. *This kid can help me.*

Chapter 23

Jimmy was in one of his dark moods. His life was never a happy one, even at the best of times. But, once in a while, Jimmy found himself hating something with a passion. It might be a person, life in general or a situation. When this happened, whatever he was focused on received his full attention. Freddy and Dusty avoided being around Jimmy when he was like this. They had been the casualties of Jimmy's emotional explosions. Unfortunately for them, the transformation started in a quiet and unobtrusive way. It then escalated into an explosive blast. Freddy and Dusty found it difficult to sense when Jimmy entered into this state. By the time it was obvious Jimmy was glowing with hatred, almost ready to burst. He usually wanted someone to be with him. Trying to escape was difficult and dangerous.

The Strand was the closest Jimmy usually allowed himself to be to the beach and the ocean, he dreaded so much. He, Dusty and Freddy were now sidling along The Strand. It was late afternoon. Freddy was next to Jimmy and noticed something out of the corner of his eye. Jimmy increased his pace and his movements became more animated.

Freddy nudged Dusty to get his attention.

"Uh oh," said Freddy.

Dusty looked up at Freddy and saw what was going on. He could plainly see Jimmy churning along with a crazed look in his eyes. Jimmy saw a bench and grabbed his partners by the arm. They both became nervous as he steered them to the empty seat and pushed them down. Neither said a word. Jimmy stood looking down on them, radiating anger. His fists were clenched and his face was red.

"I've been thinkin' about that fuckin' surfer," yelled Jimmy.

"Yeah, yeah. He's an asshole," Freddy chimed in.

"He needs to be shown. He needs to learn that he can't fuck with me. We're going to figure out a way to get him, right now."

"Uh, okay Jimmy. Yeah man. We can help," said Dusty.

"Well, give me some fuckin' ideas then. I want him fucked up bad," said Jimmy.

"We could jump him and beat him up. We could get him on the beach in front of everybody," said Freddy.

"I don't go to the beach. Anyway, he might have fuckin' friends there," hissed Jimmy.

"We could tell people he's a homo and a wimp and that he tried to kiss you," said Dusty.

"I have a better idea. We know a lot of badass guys, don't we? We'll tell them all something about surfer Brett that will piss them off. Whatever they hate, that's what we'll tell them. He'll have a shit storm coming at him from all directions."

"Fuck yeah," yelled Freddy

A few people stopped on The Strand and looked at the three miscreants. Dusty smiled in relief, hoping that this pronouncement would end the discussion and make Jimmy happy.

"This is what I want you guys to do. Call whoever you can think of. But make sure they are bad dudes. Tell them that fuckhead Brett Sloan is saying bad things about them or is going to turn them in to the police. Whatever will piss them off," said Jimmy.

"Yeah, okay," said Dusty.

"I'm on it," said Freddy.

Jimmy smiled as he envisioned Brett being hassled and beat up by the meanest young criminals in El Porto.

"He won't know what hit him," said Jimmy.

Chapter 24

Brett opened the door to the Stephens home. It was starting to cool off after a scorching midday. He was thankful to have a place to get out of the hot sun that was so close to the beach. *Man, I'm sure glad I didn't have to walk up that steep hill to my house. Now, I think I'll head down to 43rd street and go in the water.* As he walked down The Strand toward the Tiki Hut, two rough looking young men appeared, one on each side and a bit behind. Brett didn't notice them right away as he thought how pleasant the water would feel. The two kept pace with him but said nothing. Brett was startled out of his thoughts by the taller of the two, leaning into and bumping him into the other, shorter man. The shorter man pushed Brett back into his partner.

"Stop pushing me shithead," said the taller man.

Brett was surprised and intimidated by these young men who he guessed were in their early twenties. He looked at the taller one who was skinny with stringy brown hair, and a vacant look in his dark eyes. The shorter one had a swastika tattoo on one arm and black hair. His eyes displayed aggressive and violent emotions. He seemed like a spring that was wound much too tight.

"Uh, er, uh. I didn't mean to. Sorry," said Brett.

"If you keep fucking with us, we'll beat the shit out of you," said the short one.

Brett was pinned between them with few options. *These guys are really pissed about something. But what?* Brett started walking a bit faster but his captors kept pace. He felt trapped and afraid. Brett tried to focus on his options. *I better do something or these guys will hurt me. Maybe I can run.*

"Uh hey, I didn't mean anything," said Brett.

"Are you Brett Sloan? Brett Sloan the shithead?" snarled the tall one.

"Uh, yeah. That's me," Brett replied.

"Hey Tanner. I think he's flipping us shit. Don't you?"

The taller one inched closer and leaned again. The shorter one grabbed his arm. Brett noticed he had a wide scar on his cheek.

"My name is Bill Hasty and my friend is Tanner Brown. I heard you bin saying stupid shit about me. That's not good for you Brett."

Brett tensed and tried to pull his arm away from Bill Hasty causing Tanner to grab the other arm.

"Hey. I don't even know you guys. I haven't said anything to anybody. Why would I?" whined Brett.

"We heard you bin spreading rumors about a lot of our friends too," said Tanner.

Brett was now becoming fearful like a trapped, feral animal.

"I mind my own business. No way I did that," protested Brett.

As Bill and Tanner started to pull Brett away from The Strand, a group of teenagers walked toward them. Brett recognized them as surfers he knew. He started to thrash against his captors.

"Leave me alone. I didn't do anything," he yelled.

The surfers ran toward Brett. The two criminals let him go but stood their ground, surveying the new development.

"Is there a problem, Brett?" asked one of the surfers.

Brett trotted away from the two hoodlums.

"Yeah. They think I've been saying stuff which I haven't. I don't even know these guys," said Brett.

Some of the surfers recognized Bill Hasty and knew that he had just gotten out of jail. Nobody made a move.

"Just remember. If you fuck with us, we fuck with you surfer boy," said Bill Hasty.

Brett and his rescuers slowly backed away.

"I don't mess with anybody," said Brett.

As Brett and the group walked toward the Tiki Hut, one of the surfers turned to Brett.

"Man, you don't want to piss that guy off. He's a bad dude. He just got out of jail. What the hell was that about?"

"I don't know. He said I was saying bad stuff about him and I don't even know who he is," said Brett.

~~~

Brett sat on a bench in front of the Tiki Hut and thought about what had just happened. *Why the hell were those guys so mad at me? First I messed up the date by making Janey cry. And, now this. My summer is turning to crap.* The beach was emptying out as Brett walked toward the water. Lifeguard Bob was pulling down the black ball flag and surfers were paddling toward the waves. *Crap, I don't even feel like surfing and it looks pretty good.* After waving to Lifeguard Bob he waded into the water hoping to relax. He still remembered the helpless feeling of being trapped between two nasty looking criminals. *What if they had pounded on me? They looked a lot meaner than Jimmy.*

Brett was letting the pull of the mild undertow move him toward the waves. He maneuvered to a spot where he was out of the way of the surfers. As a medium sized wave formed he saw a surfer paddle into it. Brett watched as the wave with rider passed on the side of him. By luck he turned toward the shore to see the end of the ride but was stunned by what he saw. A long board was airborne and flying at him. He scrambled to pull himself under and barely made it before the board hit the water above him. *This can't be an accident. I better get outta here.* As he waded toward the shore someone behind him yelled.

"Fuck you Sloan. Watch your back. We're coming."

Brett, who was now shaken, did watch his back as he walked home. For the first time in his life, the world seemed mean and sinister. He smiled in relief as he neared home and safety. All of a sudden, two teenagers jumped from the shadows of an apartment building and tried to tackle Brett to the pavement. As he wrestled with them, a punch hit his ear and another hit his lip causing it to crack. He was saved only because he was already paranoid from his previous encounters. He reacted like he was going to be killed and

127

flailed his arms at his attackers. It was just enough to gain separation which allowed him to sprint up the street the short distance to his home.

Brett sat in his bedroom panting and bleeding. Luckily his injuries were not that extensive. However, his emotional state was in an uproar. *What the hell is going on? And, what am I going to do?*

Chapter 25

It was late in the day and Brett was lolling around in the apartment. Earlier, he started to become drowsy and knew that he needed a nap. After sleeping for three hours, he was slowly moving toward wakefulness with the help of a late afternoon cup of coffee. Brett had no desire to take the long walk down Kelp Street to the beach because he knew that he would have to walk back up later in the day. The phone rang.

"Yeah," said Brett.

"Hey Dude. You have to come down," said Greg Stephens.

"Why," asked Brett.

"Alan Jones has the football and he is headed to the beach in front of my house. Come on. We have to go down."

Brett thought about Alan Jones who lived near him with his wife. Still a young man, he was an ex-athlete whose brother was a pro football player. Sometimes he played around with the local kids on the beach. Although Brett was tempted to go, he was still not very awake.

"Uh, yeah, uh," mumbled Brett

"Dude, have to get your butt down here. How about this? You can stay overnight at our house. We can watch TV and play poker," said Greg.

Brett took a gulp of his coffee and thought about his offer. Usually he had a great time with Greg and his brother. Also, he always liked hanging out with Alan Jones.

"Okay. I'll be there as soon as I can," said Brett.

"Awesome dude. We'll be on the beach."

After leaving a note for Ann and putting some clothes in a bag, Brett took off. Soon he was on The Strand looking toward the beach. A group of about thirteen kids was running around with one adult who seemed bigger than life. He was not that tall but had the

129

stout look of a superior athlete. Brett left his bag by the front door of the Stephens home and ran down to the beach. Alan Jones was holding a football in one hand and waving his opposite arm at the motley group of kids who were running in the opposite direction. Greg and Brett were the oldest of the group with kids in a range of ages. The youngest was about eight. The group kept running down the beach away from Alan, who kept waving and yelling.

"Back, back, keep going."

The group trudged, in ankle deep sand, away from the athletic dynamo. To Brett, it seemed like they were running much too far. Then he saw Alan Jones throw the football. The brown cylindrical, ball shot from his arm as if it was shot out of a cannon. It soared high in the air. The football seemed to hang forever before forcing the kids to run a little further to catch up with it. Although Brett had done this before, he was still amazed at how far the ball traveled. He was the fastest of the group but was barely able to reach the ball and catch it. The group ran back far enough toward Alan so that Brett could throw the ball to him. Then, they repeated the same scene many times, allowing different kids to catch the ball. After a time, the group formed a makeshift team where the athletic man took hikes from the smallest kid and threw passes to the others. Time flew by and soon it was almost dark.

"Okay, guys. It's time to go home. We don't want your mothers getting mad," said Alan Jones.

"Thanks Mr. Jones," said one of the kids .

"Hey, Brett, stick around for a few minutes. I want to talk to you," said Alan.

After the other kids were gone Brett and Greg stood with Alan. Brett was surprised to see that he was a bit taller than the friendly, robust man. After his athletic display, Brett saw him as larger than life. Alan looked directly into Brett's eyes causing him to feel a sense of strength and safety. Greg was also in awe that Alan Jones would want to talk to his best friend.

"Brett, I think you know I do a lot around football. One thing is to help with coaching the high school team. So, I know a lot of kids," said Alan.

"Yeah, I figured that Mr. Jones," said Brett,

"Hey, I'm not your coach, at least not yet. You can call me Alan."

"Uh, okay Alan," said Brett.

"I just wanted to tell you how impressed I am with what you did for Tommy Burns. His big brother Eric told me about it. Eric is the best lineman on our team," said Alan.

Greg was now grinning in anticipation. His face displayed extreme pride. Brett, on the other hand, looked a bit confused.

"Uh, who is that? I don't know what you are talking about," asked Brett.

"Didn't you save Tommy from drowning not that long ago?"

"Oh, you mean Shorty. That's what I call him. Yeah, he was floating out to sea. It turned out okay though."

Greg looked at his friend and slapped him on the back causing him to cough.

"Well, his family wants you to know how appreciative they are," said Alan.

"I'm glad I could help," said Brett.

Alan Jones tossed the football to Brett and trotted toward The Strand.

"You guys take it easy. I like seeing you kids doing good things and staying out of trouble," he said.

Brett threw the ball to him as Greg pounded him on the back again.

"Dude, dude! You're a hero and you act like it's no big deal," asked Greg

"Hey, it wasn't that big of a deal. Lifeguards do it all the time," said Brett.

"Well I know one thing. When Janey found out the other night she looked at you like you were Superman."

"Whatever. You don't need to make it more than it is," said Brett

"Man, can that guy throw the pigskin or what?" asked Greg.

"I heard he played football at some college and his brother is in the pros. What an arm," said Brett.

When the boys walked into the Stephens home, the fragrant odor of spaghetti sauce was flowing out of the kitchen. Brett was overcome with hunger. Jennifer Stephens was scurrying around the kitchen in a flowered apron.

"Hi boys. Dinner will be ready in about ten minutes," she yelled.

"That's great Mom. We're starving. Brett's with us," said Greg.

"There's enough food. And, I talked to Brett's mother. When were you going to ask me if he could stay over?" she inquired.

"Oops, I guess I forgot that part."

"It's okay this time. He can stay over, but don't do that again. Ask first. I don't like getting calls from mothers when they know more about what's going on in my house than I do."

"Okay Mom. Guess what. Brett is a hero," said Greg.

"What does that mean, honey?" asked Jennifer

"Well, I forgot to tell you before. He saved Tommy Burns from drowning. Mr. Jones said that the family was really appreciative."

"Well Brett, I think that is wonderful. I will tell your mother because I doubt that you have. I know she will be very proud," said Mrs. Stephens.

The boys wolfed down the food, as soon as it was placed on the table, much to the dismay of Jennifer Stephens. She knew how teenage boys could be, however, and kept the scolding to a minimum. After dinner the three boys played poker on a table in the rec room, using plastic chips. Greg knew much more about card games than the other two. Although Greg suggested using pennies, nickels and dimes, neither Brett nor Bobby had any money, small change or otherwise. The three played different variations of poker including stud and draw. Greg, who tired of playing the same game for any length of time, changed often. Brett had only played poker a few times and did not understand it well. As soon as he started to understand the rules of one game, Greg was trying to explain to them the rules of another. *I wonder if Greg is making up the rules as he goes? It sure seems like he is winning a lot*, thought Brett. *No way I would bet real money with him.* After about an hour Greg had a large pile of chips, Brett had a few and Bobby had none. After starting to nod off Bobby said, "I'm going to bed. I don't have any chips anyway."

After Bobby left, Brett and Greg watched TV. It was always special for Brett to watch a color television after the small black and white he had at home. It was as if he was seeing a whole new world.

After some time, Brett asked Greg to turn down the television.

"Something weird happened the other day. I had all these guys hassling me," said Brett.

"What guys?"

"Well, it seemed like everywhere I went guys were threatening me or trying to fight me. I don't even know who they are."

"Did they say anything?"

"They said I was saying bad stuff about them. They all reminded me of juvenile delinquents but some were older," said Brett.

Greg thought for a minute.

"I bet I know why," he said.

"I'm glad someone does."

"I think you really pissed off Jimmy the other day. He probably tried to increase the odds for himself by getting other assholes to hassle you. That guy never forgets stuff."

"I thought that was over with. Crap, he has half of the criminals in El Porto after me."

"Watch your back Dude. Watch your back."

Chapter 26

Brett sat next to Donny looking at Mr. Potter. It was the last day of summer school. Brett was more confident than he had ever been, before a final exam. He thought about his study habits and approach, before being tutored by Donny Head, and laughed. He thought about the deal they made at the beginning of summer school. At the time, Brett felt that the ride to school and home was the most important part of the agreement. After allowing Donny to tutor him, he had changed his mind. For Brett, there was no longer a mystery or challenge associated with Algebra. He had aced all homework and every exam. He felt like he knew enough to write the final exam that he would be taking, in a few minutes. It was all because of the help he received from nerdy Donny Head. Brett smiled with confidence.

Mr. Potter scanned the classroom with a serious look.

"I hope you all studied hard for this exam. It will be one half of your grade. Please, no talking or looking," he said

Brett doubted there were any cheaters in the class because it was half the size from when they started. As he mentally prepared to take the exam, he resisted thinking about the sun outside and what he was missing. One important thing he had learned was that there was a different way of thinking when taking an exam. It was like putting on a uniform and becoming super competitive. *I need to focus and shut out everything but the test*, he thought. He was already building up to that moment when he would block out the world and block out daydreams. Brett appreciated the diminutive, pale-looking boy named Donald Head sitting next to him. *Man, I really got the better end of that deal*, he thought. Brett hoped that Donny had benefited also. In the past Brett thought of college as a vague extension of high school where study was an optional activity. Now, he understood exactly what steps he needed to take to achieve success.

"Hey, Brett, do you have any questions before this thing starts?" asked Donny.

"Uh, no, I've got it handled," answered Brett.

"That's good. Now remember. Don't hurry. And, when you are done, go back over every question."

"I already know that Donny. I haven't missed a problem yet."

"In the final, all these teachers like to throw in something really hard. Usually it's something you never use or think about."

"Okay brainiac. I'll remember," said Brett

Mr. Potter gave instructions, and the final began. The classroom was silent while most of the students struggled through the exam. Once Brett was able to refocus from his conversation with Donny, he moved smoothly through the questions. Brett found that Donny had been right again. One of the problems was not only obscure but the wording was tricky, also. Brett took his time with that problem on his second time through the test. After taking much more time than on the other problems, he understood what the answer was. Brett finished his test before anyone except Donny, who had finished in about fifteen minutes. On the last page of the exam paper was a note which said 'Brett, please stay after class.' Brett groaned quietly. He did not want to stay inside any longer than necessary.

"Hey Donny. I need to stay after. I am not sure why," said Brett.

"I'll wait outside," said Donny.

Brett waited at his desk while everyone else, including a wide-eyed Donald, filed out of the room. *What the hell do I need to stay late for? I know this crap now,* thought Brett.

"Mr. Sloan. Thank you for staying."

"Is something wrong?" Brett asked.

"You have done well on all of the exams. As a matter of fact the only student who has done better is Donald. I am very impressed. I expect your score on the final will also be good. However, I cannot give you the "A" that you deserve."

"Why not?" muttered Brett who was now really worried.

"You have missed many more days than are allowed in this class. According to the rules, I should fail you."

"But I passed everything?" he whined.

"Your grade is a B minus and I shouldn't even do that. Try to show up more often in future classes and consider yourself lucky," Mr. Potter said sternly.

In the past Brett would have considered this event to be another time when he was getting screwed. However, after learning from Donny, he now had the ability to put himself in the teachers place. Instead of looking at Mr. Potter like an enemy, he saw this as a gift.

"Thanks Mr. Potter. I really appreciate you doing this for me," said Brett.

"You are welcome Mr. Sloan."

Donny was waiting at the car in a nervous snit.

"What happened? Did you pass? Is everything okay? Tell me. Tell me," said Donny.

"I lucked out. He said I missed too many classes and I should have failed. But he let me off with a B minus," said Brett.

"Oh, is that all? Good. I would have flipped out if you had failed."

"Yeah, me too. Listen, I want to thank you for your help. You really woke me up with the tutoring," said Brett.

~~~

Ann Sloan was in the kitchen cooking macaroni and cheese. As usual she was happy that she and Brett would eat together. Many nights Brett made himself a TV dinner or two. The thick smell of cooking food kept Brett a little on edge. He couldn't wait to eat. *Man, am I getting tired of TV dinners*, he thought. Brett walked into the kitchen.

"Did you wash your hands?" asked Ann.

"Oh, I'll do that now," said Brett.

After eating a large helping of macaroni and tossed green salad, Brett went for more.

"Tell me what you have been doing. How did summer school go?" said Ann.

"I got a B minus, but I should've gotten an A."

"You know how important good grades are. Why did you only get a B minus? I know that smart young man has been helping you."

"Mr. Potter said I missed too many days. I did great on all of the tests. I think the rule is stupid. If I know the answers, I should get the grade. But at least he didn't fail me. I'm happy about that."

"We have talked about this before. You need to stay focused on school so you will get into college. It's hard to qualify without good grades. You're smart Brett, but you must follow the rules just like everyone else."

"After learning from Donny, I know a lot more about how to do schoolwork. I know if I work at it I can do alright," said Brett

Ann was satisfied that her son was on the right track and changed the subject.

"What else have you been up to?" she asked.

"You know surfing and the beach," said Brett.

Ann's eyes brightened and she smiled a bit.

"What about your date. Greg's Mom liked the girls you were with."

"It wasn't a date. And, uh...,er, I don't know how it went. It seemed okay but at the end it got weird. I like Janey but girls are hard to figure out," said Brett.

Ann started cleaning up the kitchen.

"Besides, what girl would want me as a boyfriend, anyway?" said Brett.

"Oh, you might be surprised," Ann replied.

Chapter 27

Brett was walking home after a day at the beach. Janey and the date weighed heavily on his mind. He had not tried calling Janey or seen her at the beach. He knew that it had not ended well but didn't know how bad it had been. Greg Stephens was vague in his answer, when Brett asked him about it. He only said that it was too early to tell. Brett was beginning to worry that Janey hated him. *If she does hate me, I doubt that Stacy will be much help either*, he thought.

When Brett turned left The Strand and headed up the hill toward his house, he saw something flash out of the corner of his eye. As he turned, three older boys came running toward him. They appeared vicious and determined. *Oh no, not again. I thought this was over with. I don't think these guys are willing to talk, either.*

Brett turned and ran, stubbing his toe in the process. His flip-flops slapped furiously as he sprinted away from his pursuers. He exited the street as an evasive tactic and ran between apartment buildings. When he reached another street he turned to see if he was in the clear. One thug was a few feet behind him running at full speed. Brett reacted by sticking out a leg and pushing the red-faced, sweaty aggressor, causing him to fall to the pavement. The two other attackers were close. Brett's toe was bleeding causing one flip-flop to become slippery. He ran again, barely escaping. Now, he was running up hill and separating himself from the group following him. *I better get off of the street and lose these guys.* When Brett again ducked between two houses, he slipped out of his bloody flip-flop, hitting his already stubbed toe and fell. He hit hard on the concrete walkway. In seconds the three hoodlums were on top of him.

"This will teach you to fuck with us," said one.

Brett curled on the ground with his hands over his face and head as he was hit and kicked from all sides. He tried to roll away from the blows but was surrounded. Brett was able to kick back and by sheer luck, hit one of his attackers, but was getting beaten badly.

Just when the world started spinning and he thought he was going to pass out, the attack stopped. Brett was able to lift his bruised head and see his attackers trotting away. Through a haze of pain, he thought he saw someone else in the other direction, but by the time he recovered enough to get up, no one was there. *I better get out of here before they come back.* The battered teenager slowly trudged up Kelp St. He did not have enough energy or will to watch for other attackers.

It took what little strength he had left, to walk up the hill, which now seemed like a mountain. His nose was bleeding and numerous body parts were starting to swell. He hoped that he could make it home to safety and rest.

When he finally walked into the little apartment, Ann was distraught. Brett had no strength to answer her questions, so she nuresed his wounds. After his mother had done her best to make Brett comfortable, she cried silently. Brett slowly walked to his bedroom and collapsed on his bed. His entire body was one large universe of pain. It was impossible for him to organize his thoughts. He envisioned unknown assailants, waiting in dark places to hurt him again. Just before he fell into a fitful sleep he remembered something. *Why did those guys take off? Was there really someone there?*

Chapter 28

It had been three days since the attack. Brett was still healing, mentally and physically. Nobody had called which was unusual. Ann was about to leave for work.

"Honey, I still think we should have called the police. I am scared for you," said Ann.

"I think that would be the worst thing. These guys think I am trying to get them in trouble. I'm not, but if we get the police into it, I think it will just get worse."

"I don't know how it can be worse. I have to go. Please stay in the apartment. You are not fully recovered yet."

"I will. I have to find out if I am still on somebody's black list," said Brett.

Brett lazed around the apartment but was aching to get outside. *I am so sick of TV and reading books. Crap, I need to get outta here.* Also, he was lonely. While recovering from his injuries, he had not thought about his friends or Janey but now he was wondering why he hadn't heard from anyone. *I wonder if they know what happened to me?*

After calling many times, Greg Stephens called back. He was reserved and seemed distant which irritated Brett.

"So, those guys came after you again?" asked Greg.

"Yeah but it was different guys. They got me pretty good. I am starting to wonder if it will ever end."

"Well, I don't know what to say. It's awfully hard to go up against all the bad guys in El Porto."

Brett was now starting to feel abandoned by his best friend. It sounded to him like Greg was not going to help him in any way, not even give moral support. *I better talk about something else. This isn't helping.*

"Uh, did you hear anything else about the date? I didn't mean to screw it up," asked Brett.

"Yeah, well about that. Uh, er."

"Well what?" interrupted Brett.

"Stacy is really mad at you and Janey is like really depressed, I guess."

"Maybe I should call Janey and apologize?"

"Uh, I don't know about that. Stacy said Janey never wants to see you again. I guess she thought you guys had something special and then you walked away like she wasn't important."

"What do you think I should do?" asked Brett.

"Well, with getting beat up and girl problems, maybe you should lay low. You know, let things settle down a little."

"Crap, I can't just stop living. I bet Stacy is telling everybody, she knows, that I'm a jerk, too," cried Brett.

"Listen, Stacy and I are together. Don't start putting her down," yelled Greg.

"Oh, I see. It's her or me. Well, I can see there is no way you side with me against your stupid girlfriend."

"Screw you Brett."

Brett hung up in anger and frustration as he pounded his fists on the kitchen table. His physical bruises seemed minor compared to the emotional anguish he was feeling. *Nobody likes me anymore. How did this happen? It's like everything got all screwed up. And, Greg thinks I should just give up and hide in the house all day. At least Donny the nerd thinks I'm okay.*

Brett dialed Janey's number and Janey answered.

"Hi Janey. This is Brett. Can we talk?"

After a few moments another, familiar, voice came on the line.

"This is Stacy. She doesn't want to talk to you. Just leave her alone."

"But I can explain. I didn't mean to hurt her feelings."

Brett thought he heard crying in the background.

"Don't even try. You had your chance and you blew it. After this no girl will want to go out with you," said Stacy.

"Come on Stacy. Lighten up. Can't we work this out," pleaded Brett.

"I can't believe that you're Greg's friend. Goodbye forever. Don't call again," snapped Stacy.

Well, I guess I was right about Stacy. She's probably telling everyone that I hurt Janey. And, she is probably telling Greg to avoid me, too.

Brett sat stunned. He thought about his situation. His reputation was probably destroyed, he had hoodlums after him and the first girl he really cared about wouldn't talk to him. He thought of the harsh words with Greg Stephens and Stacy. As he wondered how his life would ever improve, one small tear formed in his left eye causing him to blink. A river of tears followed.

Chapter 29

Brett was healthy, rested and bored. He had given in to his mother's request to stay in the apartment until she was sure that he was healed. But, now he was ready to face the world. He looked out the window at the sunshine streaming in. The experience of being stalked and beaten had made him cautious but not defeated. He remembered Greg's advice to lay low and became irritated. It was not in his nature to sit in an apartment all day in fear. *I am not going to hide in the house. Screw all of them. I don't care what happens.* Brett was now wondering who his true friends were and was not ready to hang out at 43rd St. where he might run into Greg, Stacy or Janey. *I'll see them soon enough.*

He left the house determined to face whatever came his way. *I've run for the last time. If I go down, I will be fighting back.* Once the decision was made, Brett mentally prepared for battle. *I better wear tennis shoes just in case. Fighting in flip-flops isn't any good.* When he reached The Strand, he headed toward Manhattan Beach Pier which was in the opposite direction of 43rd St.. He soon found a deserted patch of beach and walked toward the water. Now that Brett had made up his mind that he would not live in fear, he did not think about his enemies at all. To him, all of the external world could come at him like a huge, thick wave. He would do whatever he could to survive the onslaught. His first emersion in the ocean was thrilling. He felt that he knew what a fish felt like after flipping around on the deck of a boat, finally able to bounce back into the sea.

The day moved at a slow pace with nobody around to talk or listen to. Much as it had been at home, he was left with only his thoughts to keep him company. Although being out in the sun and floating in the sea lifted his spirits, something was missing. For the first time in his life, Brett was lonely. Toward the end of the day he walked and thought. The water lapped at his legs as he tried to assess and fix his situation. As always, when he thought about girls, he felt like a dense fog covered the secrets that he wanted to understand. It was as if the entire female population conspired to keep him misinformed and looking stupid. He was reminded about the delicacy of dealing with girls when he recalled the phone conversation with Greg. *I never thought a girl would make Greg pissed off at me. Crap, this is all turning out bad, really bad.*

As Brett walked back on The Strand, he thought about Janey. He knew that he would not feel right until he worked it out with her. Having her mad at him was not something he could stand. *I better apologize or something, even if she doesn't like it. Maybe I can talk to her without Stacy there.* Brett was nearing the bottom of Kelp St. when he spotted two scraggly looking teenagers staring at him. *One of those guys beat me up before!* He tensed in preparation for a fight. When the taller hoodlum started toward Brett he stopped and faced them and clenched his fists. The other young enemy put out his arm stopping his partner. After a few words they turned and walked away. *I wonder why that happened. Well, at least I can walk home in peace.*

Chapter 30

Brett and Donny Head stood at the front door of the Stephens home. It was late afternoon. Bobby Stephens answered the door.

"Hi Brett. Come on in," said Bobby.

Brett had no desire to see Greg. He wanted to make this as quick and painless as possible.

"Hey Bobby, I just need to get my board. I'll be quick," said Brett.

"Uh okay, Brett."

They walked into the rec room where Greg Stephens was lounging on the couch. He sat up when they entered. When he saw who it was, he frowned. Before he could say anything, Brett said, "I am just getting my board. I'll be gone in a minute."

Brett and Donny walked across the room toward the back of the house. Donny knew something wasn't right and wanted to keep moving. Greg did not budge from the couch but Bobby walked with them. Brett turned to Bobby.

"This is Donny. He helped me with algebra in summer school. I'm going to give him some tips on surfing."

Bobby looked at Donny who wore white swim trunks and a bright red T-shirt. He smiled slightly.

"Hi Donny. I'm Bobby. That's my brother Greg in the other room. Have you been in the ocean much?"

"Uh, hi. I don't go to the beach very often. I know how to swim though."

"Well, it's a lot different than the pool. I guess if you are going to do this, Brett is a good guy to show you."

"I'm going to get my board and head out," said Brett.

"See you around," said Bobby.

Brett and Donny trudged across the empty beach toward the water. Brett did not want a crowd of people watching the lesson.

This was a first for both of them. Donny had his skinny arms around Brett's board as he struggled to carry it. Brett resisted the urge to do it himself. He felt it was important for his friend to do everything. After what seemed like hours, the board lay on the sand next to the lifeguard tower and Donny rested.

"Whew. That was heavier than I expected," said Donny

"Yeah, you better rest a little," said Brett.

"It seemed sort of tense back at the house. What's going on?"

"Well, I thought Greg was my best friend but now he has Stacy. We had words about a double date that didn't go so well."

"Yeah life isn't always easy. My dad told me that he gave up trying to figure out women. He just plows ahead and hopes for the best."

"I guess if it's a choice between doing nothing and plowing ahead, I'll plow ahead," said Brett.

"Yeah, doing nothing is like dying, I guess," said Donny.

"Okay, Donny. That's enough about my problems. A lot of learning how to surf, is understanding the ocean and waves. The first thing we need to do is get you in the water. Leave the board and follow me."

Once the two were in the water, Brett gave Donny a little time to adjust to this new environment. They were not far out but Donny was nervous. Nothing in his short, sheltered life had prepared him for noisy, crashing waves, white water and undercurrents. The only reason Donny did not go for shore was that Brett was by his side. Brett experienced how Donny approached training him and had formulated a simple plan. When he thought about the steps, he realized that even though something was clear in his mind, it had to be absorbed in small, incremental steps by his student. That is how Donny taught Brett algebra. Brett knew that the simplest skills needed to be mastered, in order for a foundation to be formed.

Once Donny seemed more relaxed, Brett proceeded to show him how to traverse the waves without a surfboard. He demonstrated to Donny how to hold his breath while diving under incoming waves, and using the sandy bottom to his advantage. As Donny adjusted to this new environment, Brett explained how a wave formed, broke and the whitewater that continued toward the shore behind the open face. With each repetition, Donny became more relaxed and enthused. With each small triumph, the skinny nerd saw new vistas open to him.

"I think I am starting to understand, but I have a question. Why are the waves breaking in different parts? On TV they break across ," asked Donny.

"The main two reasons are the sandy bottom and the onshore wind. The sandy bottom changes all the time. If the bottom is formed in a certain way, the waves break better. If the wind blows out to sea or offshore it holds the waves up. But, if it blows toward land or onshore, it makes different parts of the waves break at the same time. We call that being 'blown out' or 'closed out' like it is now," said Brett.

"Wow, you know a lot about this stuff," said Donny.

"You know, it's not like in the surfing movies with great waves all the time. We have a lot of time to figure things out while we wait for good waves. And, when you get in a tight spot you really start to learn fast," said Brett.

"So, when do I get on the board?" asked Donny.

"We aren't going to do much with the board on the first lesson. I think if you can learn to body surf, a little, that will be good. You can't surf unless you know about the ocean," said Brett.

"Okay, Brett. I can see that there's more to this than I thought."

Brett then explained the basics of body surfing and had Donny move toward shore and watch while he demonstrated. After a few awkward attempts and some correcting words, Donny was able to push into a wave, put his head down with arms at his side, and body surf halfway to the shore. His skinny body popped out of the water, with arms raised, as if he had won the Olympics. *Wow! Donny is starting to lose his fear. This is great!,* thought Brett.

"Yah did good Donny. Yah did good," yelled Brett.

"Can't I go on the board? I carried that big thing all the way down here," begged Donny.

Brett grinned at the enthusiasm of his first student. Also, he was surprised at his own success, and felt that he had gained as much as Donny.

"Let's go up and get that board Donny," said Brett.

"Yaaaaaayyyy," yelled Donny.

Once they were back in the water, Brett got on the board and talked about the importance of balance. He demonstrated paddling with both arms. Donny was soon lying on top of the board. To Brett he seemed tiny on the large Styrofoam and fiberglass structure.

"Now listen to me. I am going to push you into some whitewater. I don't want you to stand up yet. That is for later on. Just hold on and ride the whitewater on your stomach. Okay," said Brett.

"Okay Brett."

Brett, who was waist high, moved toward the setting sun. He pulled Donny and the board along with him. He smiled as a larger wave broke creating a wall of foamy, whitewater.

"Hold on Donny. Here it comes," yelled Brett.

When the whitewater neared, Brett pushed board and rider toward the shore. Both were pulled forward as the board was caught by the incoming surge. Brett heard a scream of joy from his friend as he rode on his first wave. *Well, I guess it doesn't take much for Donny to get stoked*, thought Brett.

Chapter 31

Janey's mother called up to her from the living room. She was at her usual place, lying on the bed reading a book. She was hibernating. Since the date, life had seemed colorless and the future lacking in potential.

"Janey, it's Stacy again. She said you won't answer the phone. Come on, you have been moping for too long. Stacy thinks that you hate her now."

Janey put down her book and sat up. She grabbed the light purple princess phone and dialed.

"Hi Cuz. I'm not mad at you. I'm just depressed," said Janey.

"Oh Janey. I'm happy you called. I thought because I told Brett to never call again, I was in trouble," said Stacy.

"No, I blame myself. I practically attacked Brett on our first date. And, then I got mad at him when it didn't go that well. I bet he thinks I am a crazy girl," moaned Janey.

"Well, I think you just showed how much you like him, that's all. You are too good for him. If he just splits after a little kissing, I would forget him."

"I don't want to forget about him but I don't want to be rejected either."

"Well if you really feel that way then it might help if you took Brett's calls. I know he's been calling even after I told him not to."

"I feel like I might say something stupid if I talk to him. Or worse I might cry."

"Remember, you will meet other guys even if it doesn't work out with him. Some guys don't want to have a girl friend. I think Brett is one of them. He likes you but he doesn't want to be tied down. That's what Greg said before."

"So, what am I supposed to do? Maybe I don't want to be just friends. Maybe I want more."

"Well you can't stop living because of this. I know you like the beach and we need to go. The summer will be over before we know it. Please, please" pleaded Stacy.

"What about him? What if he's there?" asked Janey.

"You can play volleyball and go in the water. Just try to forget about it. You have to sooner or later, anyway. I can't go to the beach without my beach buddy. I need you with me."

Janey thought about the beach and all it had to offer. It was now a part of her life and she could feel its magnetic pull.

"Oh screw it. Let's go. I guess I can't stay in my room for the rest of the summer. I've already read three books," said Janey.

"Wow, this is great. Listen, I'll come over and pick you up now that I can drive. We can go eat somewhere and plan our next beach trip," said Stacy.

"Okay, see you soon," said Janey.

~~~

Later that evening Stacy called Greg.

"Hi Stace, what's goin on?" said Greg.

"Okay, here's the deal. I finally got Janey to agree to come to the beach with me, but she still has feelings for Brett."

"Yeah well, I don't know what's going on with him. We sorta had a falling out. I know you don't like him now," said Greg.

"Well sweetie, I think Janey needs me to at least get along with him. She isn't going to forget about her crush because of me."

"Let me get this straight. First he's bad because of the date but now he is okay because Janey still likes him?"

"Uh yeah, sweetie. I can't burn all my bridges."

"Alright. Let me see what I can find out. If he knew how happy we are together, maybe he would be open to seeing more of Janey."

"Oh, oh, you are sooooo sweet Greggy. You know I feel the same," cooed Stacy.

"How about this? You bring her down to the beach. If I see him I'll try to explain how sensitive she is about the date and everything. I think he is smart enough to understand. Okay?" said Greg.

"I think that will be fantastic. If it gets weird for Janey, we can just go home and regroup. Maybe he won't even be there when we are," said Stacy as if the whole issue was settled.

"Sounds good Stace. Why don't you drive down here and pick me up tonight? We can cruise around or something."

"I'll be there at eight. I am sure we can think of 'or something' to do," said Stacy.

Chapter 32

Summer school was over, the days were hot and Brett felt that he was in sync with the flow of the summer. Now that he had decided to deal with life head on, he felt empowered to overcome any difficulties. School would be starting soon and Brett was not going to waste the last days of summer brooding and sulking. Although he had not contacted Greg or Janey yet, he was intending to speak with each of them. If it didn't work out then it wasn't because he ran away.

At the end of each sun-filled day he slept, as if in a coma, with vivid dreams flowing to him like swells of water from the ocean's horizon. He tried to forget that soon school would be starting and was, for the most part, successful.

On this evening, Brett watched TV, eating Jiffy Pop popcorn while lying on the couch. The phone in the kitchen rang.

"Brett, it's for you," said Ann.

As Brett walked into the kitchen he saw that his mother had her hand over the mouthpiece of the telephone.

"Honey, it's a girl. She didn't give her name. Maybe it's the one from your date."

Brett stopped to think. *Maybe it's Janey. We can talk and get this over with. Well here goes.* Brett expected that Janey was still sensitive about how the date went. He wanted this to go well but allowed doubts to creep in to his mind. No matter how hard he tried, he could not avoid believing that he and Janey had a special connection. Also, he remembered being flustered in the back seat of the car. His desire to be with her increased with each passing second.

"Well?" asked Ann.

Brett took the phone.

"Hi, this is Brett," he said.

"Hi Brett. This is Gretchen," said a sweet and confident voice.

After focusing on what he would say to Janey, Brett struggled to put a face to the name.

"Uh, er, uh, who?" said Brett.

"You know, Palm Springs, miniature golf."

Brett was now envisioning Gretchen's smile and long, tan legs.

"Oh, that Gretchen. Wow, you surprised me. I never thought I'd talk to you again," said Brett.

"I guess you're wondering why I called?" she asked.

"You just caught me off guard. I remember the good time we had. It was great," answered Brett.

"Well I thought you might want to return the favor. I am staying at my Aunt's house in Manhattan Beach for a week. Maybe you can show me around where you live. I want to see the beach with a local, not like a tourist," said Gretchen.

This unexpected turn of events gave Brett a sense of anticipation. *Wow, this could be fun.*

"Yeah, sure. We can do that. Just tell me when."

"Well, whenever it's convenient for you Brett."

"How about the day after tomorrow? I'll give you my address and directions. What time would be good?"

"I'll be there at ten in the morning. Thanks," said Gretchen.

After Brett gave her the information and hung up, he noticed his mother sitting at the kitchen table with a curious look in her eyes. She smiled.

"Brett, you never told me how your date went. And, now this other girl calls, who you seem to know, but I have never heard of. Can't you tell me something, anything?" asked Ann.

"Uh, okay, Mom. That was a girl I met in Palm Springs. She knows Dad's girlfriend. We played miniature golf. She is visiting and wants me to show her around. She is a little older and has a boyfriend," said Brett.

"What about your date?"

"It was going okay but at the end it got weird. I think I messed it up. I don't seem to do very good with girls, usually," said Brett.

"Honey, you might find that you can do okay with girls if you just give it some time. I want you to introduce me to this girl who is visiting. What is her name?" asked Ann.

"Uh, yeah. Her name is Gretchen. I'll introduce you," said Brett.

"Maybe you don't think much is happening with you and girls but I see a trend," said Ann.

Brett looked at his mother like she was a little too curious and a bit touched.

"Oh okay, whatever you say, Mom."

The next morning Brett heard a knock on their door at 9:30 am. His mother had already left for work after spending most of the previous evening cleaning, with Brett's help. He answered and after Gretchen waved at her ride, she came in. Gretchen wore jeans and a loose fitting cotton blouse with sandals and carried a large bag. She wore little makeup but her face and tropical-sea-green eyes were accented by bright blond hair.

"I'm sorry I'm so early. We thought it would take longer to find this place, but it was really easy," said Gretchen.

"It doesn't matter. I've been up for awhile. Do you want some coffee? I just made it," said Brett.

"Yeah and we can talk a little."

After settling in with steaming coffee in front of them, Gretchen smiled.

"Well, I think this is going to be fun. Southern Cal and beach life is sorta famous. You know the Beach Boys and all that," said Gretchen.

"They come from around here. One of them lives on The Strand," said Brett.

"What is The Strand? Oh, just tell me all about everything."

Brett talked more than he ever had in his short life. As he described El Porto and the beach, Gretchen would interrupt him with pointed questions. After about an hour of talking, Brett was ready for something else.

"Well, I think I've talked enough. Do you want to get going to the beach?" asked Brett.

"Yeah, I'll change and we can go. But, where do you hang out?" she asked.

"I go to the bottom of 43rd street. We'll probably see some of my friends there," said Brett.

"Did you plan on meeting them?"

"Uh no, but we all usually end up there on a day like this."

~~~

At midday, in late August the merciless, summer sun beat down turning the sand in El Porto into a bed of hot embers. Janey and Stacy were lying on towels near the volleyball courts listening to top 40 songs emanating from a tiny, white transistor radio. Neither felt the need to talk or do much of anything. The girls noticed when the sun was blocked by something overhead. Looking up Janey saw Bethany, the tall girl who she had been playing volleyball with during the summer.

"Hi Bethany," said Janey.

"Hey, let's play. All girls this time. Some of my teammates are with me. We need one more player," said Bethany.

"Isn't the sand too hot? I feel like I could go to sleep," said Janey.

"We spray water on the sand before we start. Why don't you jump in the ocean and wake up. We'll wait," offered Bethany.

"Okay, I think it would be good to get wet and cool off."

Stacy took little notice as Janey got up and trotted toward the water trying to avoid the blistering heat of the sand. As Janey passed the lifeguard tower she bolted and dove in. It felt like her temperature dropped forty degrees which shocked her body back to life. She soon joined the other girls and started to prepare to play by hitting the ball around. Stacy started to watch the game. She noticed that Janey seemed at home and could keep up with the older girls. It was as if a switch was flipped and Janey became a complete person when she was competing.

As she watched the game, Stacy noticed Brett walking down 43rd street onto The Strand. She still had negative feelings toward him and wanted to forget he ever existed. But, she noticed something else. Stacy could not help wondering if the girl near him was somebody he knew. As they walked, it was soon apparent that they were together. Stacy's curiosity radar became active and questions raced through her head. As the two walked past the volleyball court, Janey stopped and bent down with her hands on her knees as if tired. *Uh oh. This might not be good,* thought Stacy. Janey's jaw was clenched and her face was white in spite of her tan. Janey's pinched, piercing eyes stared at the pretty, tan, blond girl in the revealing bikini, next to Brett. Neither of them seemed to notice. Janey jerked her head away and stood up straight.

"Let's finish this game and then I'm done," said Janey.

Bethany sensed that something was off with Janey and wanted to ease whatever was bothering her.

"Yeah, let's finish up. It's awfully hot," she said.

Soon Janey was standing over Stacy with a red face and angry eyes.

"Who was that with Brett?" she asked

"I don't know. Maybe they'll come over. Brett waved to me when he walked by," answered Stacy.

"I thought you knew everybody around here? I don't like her already," spit out Janey.

"Hey, don't get mad at me. Wait until you find out what the deal is before you go ballistic. I thought you didn't want to see him anyway?"

Just when Stacy thought Janey might do something extreme she saw Greg approaching. She hoped that Greg could help this situation, which called for answers.

"Hi, sweetie. Sit with us," said Stacy.

"Hey Dudettes. How goes it?" asked Greg.

"Who is that girl with Brett," asked Janey without concealing her contempt.

Greg looked at Janey and realized that she was a little pushier than usual.

"Hey, I haven't even talked to him in weeks. I have no idea who that girl is," said Greg.

"I thought you were his friend?" snapped Janey.

Greg looked at Stacy.

"Well after the date, things have been iffy."

"Really? I don't see why. What does you and Brett have to do with how the date went?" asked Janey.

Janey's focus changed when she saw Brett and Gretchen walking toward them. Gretchen was close to Brett and would touch his arm periodically, while she talked and smiled. Janey looked at Brett first and then stared at Gretchen. She leaned over and whispered to Stacy, "She's hanging all over him."

"Uh, here they are. Hi Brett. Who's your friend," asked Greg.

Brett introduced Gretchen and filled them in. When he came to Janey, she frowned and turned her head away. She said some inaudible words.

"I could get used to this beach thing. I really like it," said Gretchen.

Janey, who was now ready to yell at Gretchen, decided to remove herself from the situation.

"I better wash off. Nice meeting you," mumbled Janey.

Greg looked at Brett and winked with a knowing look toward Janey.

"Hey Brett, let's talk later. It's been awhile," he said.

Brett was sensing that he had made Janey even more upset. *At least Greg is willing to talk to me now.*

"Yeah, I'll call you later tonight. I guess we'll keep taking the tour. Seeya later" said Brett.

Gretchen was surprised that they were leaving so soon but guessed the reason why.

"Bye. Nice meeting you guys," she said.

As they quickly walked back toward The Strand, Stacy got up. She moved next to Greg.

"I'm glad that's over with. Janey isn't doing very well. And why are you talking to him at all?" asked Stacy.

Greg's frustrated look let Stacy know that she should back off.

"For one thing you asked me to talk with him. And, if you are going to have to get along with him, then I think I can talk to him, too. And, you keep asking for information. Let me deal with it. You better go see how Janey is doing," snapped Greg.

Gretchen and Brett walked along The Strand.

"So were you going to tell me what's up with that Janey girl?" she asked.

"Uh, what do you mean?" Brett replied.

"Well, she was firing bullets at me out of her eyes," said Gretchen.

"Er, uh, we went on a date with Greg and Stacy. It got sorta hot in the back seat. I guess I got nervous at the end and screwed it up. I want to apologize but she won't return my calls," said Brett.

"I bet it got hot. I'll give you a tip. That girl more than likes you. You better figure out how to deal with it."

"Hey, she acts like she doesn't want anything to do with me. I'll call her again but I doubt that it will matter."

Gretchen messed up Brett's hair with one hand and pushed his shoulder with the other, capturing his attention.

"Stupid boy. You can't just be so lazy about it. It doesn't work that way,"

Chapter 33

The sun was setting leaving streaks of purple and bright orange across the sky. The August air was motionless and hot, laying an oppressive blanket over El Porto. Jimmy, Dusty and Freddy, who were united once again, sat in their favorite dust-filled crawl space in the candlelight. Dusty had no other friends and had been relieved when Freddy told him that Jimmy was no longer mad at him. However, he trusted neither of his friends to treat him decently on a consistent basis.

"I have something here for you punks to see," said Jimmy.

"What's that?" asked Freddy.

Jimmy pulled out a switchblade knife and pushed a button. A long, shiny blade snapped out. Dusty pulled back a little in fear. After the last incident with Jimmy, on this very spot, he was a bit jumpy.

"It looks wicked. Uh, what is that for?" asked Dusty.

Jimmy's shifty eyes darted between his companions while he twisted the knife in different directions watching it shine in the light. He smiled as if envisioning something.

"You know I hate surfers. And, I hate one fuckin' surfer more than any of them. This knife is for that asshole surfer boy, Brett Sloan."

Both Freddy and Dusty perked up at the threat of violence.

"You could really hurt him with that. Are ya really gonna stick him?" asked Freddy.

"School is starting soon. I won't be there because I've been kicked out for the last time. But, they always have a stupid back-to-school dance. I say we jump him there."

"I thought he got pounded after we spread those rumors?" asked Freddy.

"Yeah he got fucked up a little but it wasn't enough. I'm gonna make him really bleed.

"Yeah, man. No way he could take on all three of us. And you have that wicked knife. We could fuck him up bad," said Dusty.

"And he deserves it after what he did to my nose," said Jimmy.

"Yeah, fuck him up, really fuck him up," said Freddy with a gleeful smile.

For the next hour the three smoked cigarettes and schemed. Jimmy sketched out a simple plan. To convince the other two of his skill, he bragged about all of the slick criminal things he had done. Freddy and Dusty became increasingly infused with a sense of power as they listened to how Jimmy would slash the unsuspecting Brett Sloan. Their bravery was bolstered by the fact that Jimmy would wield the shiny, switchblade, knife which scared both of them.

"All this talking has made me thirsty. How about some cheap red wine?" asked Freddy?

Jimmy's mouth was dry from so much talking. Wine sounded good to him.

"You got wine? Where is it?" asked Jimmy.

"At the beach," said Freddy.

"You know I hate the beach," yelled Jimmy.

"Yeah but it's night and they're having a Red Mountain fountain down past the end of The Strand. For a few bucks we can drink as much as we want and nobody will fuck with us," said Freddy.

"What is that? A Red Mountain fountain?" asked Jimmy.

"Oh, they buy a bunch of gallons of Red Mountain wine and paper cups. It's so cheap that it's like having a fountain of wine," said Freddy.

"Well, I am thirsty. I guess for some cheap wine I can go down there. When does it start?" asked Jimmy.

"In about an hour. I have two bucks. That's enough for all of us. I know the guy who is doing it. We just show up," said Freddy.

"Shit, if it's that cheap and easy, maybe we should switch over to wine," said Dusty.

"You can get some nasty hangovers from that wine, though. It's easy to drink a lot, but the next day can be bad, really bad," said Freddy.

"The price is right and we are drinking vino tonight," sang Dusty as they started crawling toward the edge of the house.

~~~

Jimmy's gang carried flashlights and nothing else. The Strand was lit but Jimmy, who had an aversion to the beach, wanted the flashlights in case of the unexpected. The three delinquents slithered down a bank of ice-plant, crossed the parking lot and walked onto the beach. The night was moonless, hot and balmy. Waves could be heard crashing in the distance causing Jimmy to feel a little queasy.

"We just head this way toward the oil pier," said Freddy

"I don't see anything that way. Are you sure?" asked Jimmy.

"Yeah, I'm sure. It's just starting. Later they will have a fire too," said Freddy.

"Those waves give me the creeps. One time when I was a kid I got pulled by an undertow. The lifeguard pulled me out but I thought I was going to die," said Jimmy.

"So that's why you hate the beach, huh?" said Dusty.

"Yeah and other shit," answered Jimmy.

The trio were well past The Strand and any houses. All three were a bit jumpy. A bit of light flickered in the distance.

"That must be them," said Freddy.

"Why are they way the hell out here?" whined Jimmy.

"Nobody will bother us out here. Like cops especially," said Freddy.

As they walked the light became brighter. When they arrived, a medium sized fire of driftwood was burning. About ten teenagers were there. Large coolers with ice contained gallon bottles of red wine.

The three stood in front of a tall, pimply-faced teenager.

"Hey Chad. We made it," said Freddy.

"Hi Freddy. Oh you brought your friends. Hey guys," said Chad.

Jimmy and Dusty nodded.

"How much do we owe you?" asked Freddy.

"Oh uh, here are some cups. You owe me fifty cents apiece for all you can handle. Pour your own. Later on I'll be pouring if you guys are too blasted," said Chad.

Jimmy, Freddy and Dusty grabbed large paper cups and filled them with wine. Jimmie sniffed his full cup and smiled. Freddy took a large gulp and grinned.

"This red vino smells sweet," said Jimmy.

"Yeah Freddy, this is going to be fuckin' awesome," said Dusty.

They drank as more people continued to appear out of the darkness. As usual, Jimmy bragged about his exploits to his friends and made sure that others could hear. Freddy and Dusty were feeling very full of themselves as the alcohol took effect. Jimmy talked non-stop and was loud. When he started to bad mouth surfers, he was interrupted.

"Hey, Jimmy. Shut the fuck up about surfers unless you want to find a fist in your face," said a tall, muscular teenager.

Jimmy, who was now inebriated but not incapacitated, jumped up and took a wide swing in the general direction of the voice. Before he knew what was happening his arm was pinned behind his back.

"Hey man. Stop it with my arm. That hurts," yelled Jimmy, causing the drunken crowd to look at him.

"I'm a surfer and I'm sick of hearing that shit coming out of your mouth Jimmy. Take your friends and go."

Freddy and Dusty looked on wide-eyed but did nothing.

"We paid our money. You can't kick us out," whined Jimmy.

The angry surfer pulled on Jimmy's arm causing him to wince in pain.

"Here's the deal asshole. Fill your cups one last time and go or I will beat the crap out you and your friends," he said.

"Okay, okay. Just let go," said Jimmy.

As the ratty group walked away with flashlights scanning across the sand, Jimmy turned back.

"Fuck you surfer boy. If I wasn't drunk I'd kick your ass."

Dusty walked a little faster and was afraid to look back.

Chapter 34

It was the first week in September. The hot, dry, stagnant, smog-filled air hung over the beach and the houses above. Brett sat in the kitchen looking at the morning paper. He was eating cinnamon toast and drinking coffee. There was no surf and he wasn't in a hurry to get down to the beach. Now that the start of school was only a few weeks away, he could not help thinking about it. Although he wanted summer to last forever, his new-found study habits gave him a sense of confidence and anticipation. *I wonder how I'll do this year.*

The ringing phone grabbed his attention.

"Hello," said Brett.

"Hi, this is Greg. I just wanted to say that I think we need to stick together. Chicks can get all spun up over stuff but that doesn't mean we have to," said Greg.

Brett was relieved that Greg was trying to close the gap between them.

"Yeah, let's forget about all of that stuff. I just want to be nice to everybody, including any girls my friends like."

"Well dude. We're about ready to head out on our vacation. I hate to be gone at the end of summer but I guess we have to go."

"Yeah, you should like it. I hear Yellowstone is nice this time of year."

"At least we'll have a few days after we get back before school starts."

"I guess you'll miss the dance, then," said Brett.

"You know, Stacy isn't too happy about that. She and Janey will be there."

Brett recalled being in the back seat so close to Janey, and kissing her. She had looked stunning sitting in a cloud of intoxicating perfume that filled the small space. He tried to stifle sexual thoughts that sprung up, with little success.

"Hey, I've changed my mind about Janey. I really like her. I guess I couldn't admit it. I am going to talk to her at the dance. I hope she listens," said Brett.

"Dude, you have a lot to learn. I think she still likes you a lot, but that thing at the beach didn't help any."

"I don't get it. Gretchen is just a friend. That's all."

"Janey has feelings for you but I think she is really emotional about it.

"All I can do is try. Maybe I'll learn as I go. But it isn't easy," moaned Brett.

"Yeah, you keep at it. Oh, whatever happened with all those guys trying to beat you up," asked Greg.

"I decided I wasn't going to run anymore. After that it just stopped but I'm not sure why," said Brett.

"That's good, even if you don't know the reason. I'll talk to you later."

"Bye."

Although Brett knew that his friend would be gone, he had forgotten about a ride to the dance. He knew his mother would take him but he didn't want that. *Maybe Donny wants to go with me*, he thought. Brett dialed Donny Head's number hoping that he was there. After a pleasant lady answered, Donny was on the phone.

"Hello, who's this?"

"Hi Donny. This is your student."

"Uh, er, uh, hi Brett. You aren't my student. I didn't help you that much," said Donny.

"Whatever. Are you going to the dance?"

"Uh, I guess so. Why?"

"Well, I thought you might want to pick me up and we could go together."

Donny smiled with excitement as he envisioned the two of them walking into the dance together. *This could be the coolest thing in my whole life. I might even dance with a girl,* he thought.

"Yeah, yeah! That would be great Brett! We can hang out together," said Donny gushing enthusiasm.

Brett thought about how much of a nerd his new friend was, but remembered how he helped with summer school. *Maybe the nerdiness will go away if he hangs out with non-nerds a little bit.*

"Okay, okay. Calm down Donny. It's not that big of a deal. Pick me up at six, okay?"

"Sure, Brett, sure. I'll be cool. See you then."

Brett enjoyed dances but he knew this one could be different. His need to clear the air with Janey made him a bit nauseous. He wondered if she would talk to him at all. *I seem to be able to hurt her without even trying. I better just let things come to me at this dance. If it gets weird I'll head the other way or leave early. Hell, Stacy will probably keep Janey away from me anyway.*

~~~

It was almost dark. Jimmy and his two partners were slinking along The Strand. In spite of Jimmy's aversion to the water he was short on cash and hoped that they could rob some unsuspecting stroller in the cover of darkness. Now that he had found out about how cheap Red Mountain wine was, he wanted to buy a few gallons for his small gang. He also liked the idea of charging money to young kids for providing them alcohol.

"Isn't it sorta open here to be robbing people?" asked Dusty.

"Shut up. We went over this. It'll be dark. We just find a good hiding place and jump out and grab some guy's wallet," said Jimmy.

"Yeah, shut the fuck up," said Freddy who was also thinking of gallons of red wine.

Jimmy spotted a light with the bulb burnt out and steered them into an alley on the side of a seemingly vacant house. He situated himself so that he could look down The Strand and got comfortable.

"Remember, Freddy and I will hit high and get him on the ground. Dusty, you grab his wallet and we run for it. I'd like to beat him up too, but we won't have time. We meet back at the hideout," whispered Jimmy.

It was not very dark and the young criminals were getting bored. Periodically, Dusty would twitch a little startling Freddy and Jimmy who would glare at him. Jimmy spotted two people in the distance strolling toward them.

"Let them go by. I will tell you when we do it. We want someone who is alone," whispered Jimmy.

They watched as the couple walked by. They were focused on each other and did not notice the three robbers lurking in the darkness.

"I see a guy down there. This is it. Remember what I said," snarled Jimmy.

A lightweight man was walking briskly by them. He seemed to be intent on moving toward his destination. When he was a bit past the lurking trio, they pounced. Jimmy and Freddy each grabbed an arm and pushed the man to the ground. The surprised victim started yelling.

"Help, help. I'm being robbed," he yelled.

Dusty tried to ignore the screams and focus on the man's wallet. Although the man was pinned to the cement, he was still moving his hips and legs trying to gain leverage. Dusty, who did not have an ounce of courage, anyway, was having a difficult time grabbing the wallet from the wriggling man.

"Grab the fuckin' wallet," yelled Jimmy.

The fear of Jimmy's wrath spurred Dusty on. He started to rapidly hit the back of the victim's slacks, hoping to find the pocket and the wallet within. By sheer luck he came up with a thick black wallet a second before the man rolled over on his back and started kicking harder. Dusty ran but said nothing. Jimmy and Freddy held on to the increasingly agitated man.

Freddy let go and bent over in pain.

"Shit, he got me in the balls," screamed Freddy.

Jimmy took a glance around and saw that Dusty was gone. He grabbed Freddy and turned to run. They both lunged forward onto the cement after being kicked from behind by the irate victim. They scrambled to their feet and raced away.

"I'll get you little punks. I'll get you," yelled the man.

Chapter 35

Stacy and Janey were relaxed in Janey's bedroom in the hot, muggy, early morning after Stacy's first sleepover. Janey wore simple, flannel pajamas and Stacy wore a sexy, feminine, black teddy. Stacy stared at Janey and frowned.

"What do you mean, you might not go to the dance?" whined Stacy.

"He'll be there. I know he will. I know he thinks I'm plain and boring compared to that girl he was with," said Janey.

"Listen, I talked to Greg about Brett. He likes you. It's just that he doesn't know how to deal with girls very well. And, we both know that can change. Sometimes it just takes a while for guys to wake up. That's all."

"He was doing fine with that blond bimbo he was with. I still can't believe how she was crawling all over him,"

"Don't you think you are being little catty? I didn't think she was that bad,"

Janey's lower lip quivered as a tear started to form in her left eye. She ignored the question.

"Do you really think he likes me? I screwed up everything on that stupid date. " asked Janey.

"The date wasn't so bad. To tell you the truth, I think he likes you more than he wants to admit. I think he's scared," said Stacy.

"So, you think I scared him off. I'm good at that," moaned Janey.

"No, no. I think he is afraid that he will lose his freedom if he likes you too much. That's all."

"Okay, I'll go to the dance. We'll see if you're right. I wonder if he'll even talk to me. "

"You know…you might think about other guys too. I'm sure that a lot of guys would like to take you out,"

"I don't care about other guys. I just care about Brett. Maybe someday I'll change but not yet."

"I am starting to wonder if he deserves you. Really, it's like he is in his own world when there is a girl that would probably die for him," said Stacy.

The girls talked about everything that had happened since Janey had moved to El Segundo. Stacy reminded Janey of how shy she was when she first arrived and how she now seemed like a local. To Stacy, her cousin had made great progress in the social scene, in spite of her romantic issues with Brett. Janey had mixed feelings about the summer and the beach scene. She had come to love going to the beach and playing volleyball in the bright sun. Also, she sensed a strong pull from the ocean and missed it when she was away for even a few days. Although she was still self-conscious, it was not nearly as bad as before. She knew that it had been good for her to be at the beach and to open up. However, to Janey, the beach would always represent Brett and her failure to connect with him.

After they had talked about the summer, Stacy smiled.

"I feel the need to do some shopping. After all, we have a dance to go to don't we?" said Stacy.

"Alright Stacy, let's go to the mall," said Janey.

Chapter 36

Brett sat in the kitchen with his mother. She smiled thinking about her handsome boy at the dance with music playing and lights flashing.

"Honey, are you going to meet a girl at the dance?" she asked.

"Uh, nope. I am going with Donny Head.

"I thought maybe you were seeing that girl from El Segundo?"

"You know, now that I am open to having her as a girlfriend, nothing seems to be happening," said Brett.

Ann knew from talking with Jennifer Stephens that Janey was still very interested in Brett, even if he couldn't figure out what to do.

"What happened with that Palm Springs girl? Did that go well?" asked Ann.

"Uh, yeah. I think she liked me showing her around. Sorry she left before you could meet her," said Brett.

"It seems that you have no trouble attracting pretty girls," said Ann.

"Mom, I think Donny is here. I gotta go. See ya later."

~~~

Brett thought about the dance as they drove toward El Segundo. Donny rambled on, but Brett barely heard what he was saying. He envisioned dancing in a dark room with a loud band playing. He remembered how pretty the girls looked when dressed up, causing him to think about physical attributes of the opposite sex. Just as he was imagining a slow dance with Janey, his mother's questions about girls, intruded into his thoughts. He could picture clearly the talkative Stacy and the athletic Janey. Although he did not consider the date with Janey a success, he craved the closeness he had with her. Before, his biggest fear was that he would be tied down. Now he wondered if he would ever be with Janey. *Man I hope she doesn't hate me. I better let her know how I really feel.*

"Hey Brett, what do you think?" asked Donny.

"Huh, what? Sorry I didn't hear what you said," replied Brett.

"I was wondering if you could introduce me to some girls?"

"Uh, oh, I guess so. I know two that you can meet, if they'll talk to me."

"That's great, really great," gushed Donny.

Brett was still far away. In his thoughts, he was holding hands with Janey who was not letting go.

It was early evening when Brett and Donny arrived at the dance which was at the El Segundo Recreation Park. The sun still shone bright and the air was balmy. "I Can't Get No Satisfaction" was blasting out from the double doors of the multi-function hall. The boys merged into the line of entering teens, passing under the sign that stated, "No entry without shirt and shoes."

Coming in from the light, Brett was surrounded by darkness so complete that he could see only specks of light moving across and over everything. As his eyes adjusted, dancing forms became visible and he was assaulted by the intoxicating mix of perfumes that permeated the hall. At one end of the hall, The Jaguars, a five-piece band dressed in matching sports coats and slacks gestured animatedly as they played. Overhead hung a large rotating globe embedded with tiny mirrors. Brett realized that it was the source of the dancing lights. Surrounded by flecks of light, in the middle of the music and crowd he felt electric, alive, as if he were swimming among brilliant eels in a hypnotic sea. Brett saw three girls dancing side by side, and moved closer. All three wore knee high skirts and long-sleeved blouses, nylons and sandals. They appeared to be practicing specific dances, something he had never considered. He stopped when he recognized the girls. Yvonne Dupree, Stacy and Janey seemed excited and happy as they tried one dance move after another.

In spite of Brett's past experience with her, it was like seeing Janey for the first time. Everything was out of focus except for her.

Brett felt a different kind of desire; a desire that focused on one person; a desire that overcame his fear of being imprisoned in a relationship. As Janey danced, with smooth athletic assurance, Brett noticed everything about her. She was much prettier than he remembered, in an all-American girl kind of way. Her shimmering hair and bright eyes radiated an inner glow. In spite of her makeup and sophisticated appearance, to Brett she was a simple un-complicated girl; a girl who was down to earth and not self-absorbed. He thought she might be the most beautiful thing he had ever seen. Wow! *It's like I never even saw her before.*

Brett's appreciation of his newfound dream girl was interrupted by a mild voice speaking under the roar of the music, directly into his ear.

"Wanna dance?"

He turned to look. The voice belonged to a girl he remembered from his English class. Brett glanced back to see Janey but she was gone. For a moment he became frantic as if his new found realization might dissipate into the room and be lost forever. When he felt the touch of the girl next to him, he instinctively nodded through his distraction.

"Okay, let's dance."

They glided into the moving mob that was in sync with the blaring music. To Brett, it was easy to overcome any shyness when the music was playing. The ebb and flow of the sound was like oceanic tides and crashing waves, to him. Still, as much as the music allowed him to escape, he could not help thinking about the Janey. *I really need to talk to her.*

After the music ended, Brett moved through the hall talking with friends and enjoying the atmosphere. He saw that Monique Dupree was attracting quite a bit of notice as usual, but did not see Janey. Brett stopped, watched and waited. When there was a break in the music, he saw Janey walking toward him. His heart beat faster with anticipation. Beads of sweat began to form on his forehead. She looked directly into his eyes, took his arm, smiled, and pulled him toward the dance floor. Surprised, he followed. *Maybe everything is alright,* he thought.

"I know our date didn't go so well. I hope we can still be friends. Will you dance with me?" asked Janey with sparkling, sultry eyes.

While waiting for the next song to begin, Janey leaned into him with a firm grasp of his arm. To Brett it was a dream come true. Her hair and light perfume were intoxicating. He leaned toward her ear to tell her that he was sorry but the music started. It was a slow dance. Janey melted into his arms as they floated amid the specks of dancing light.

"I just wanted to tell you that I'm sorry about the date. I really like you, Janey," said Brett.

She pulled him closer and smiled.

"I am enjoying dancing close like this. I could do it forever," she said.

When the music stopped, Janey backed away slightly and gently took Brett's hands. Her bright eyes bore into him causing a slight quake to move through his body. Just when Brett was about to kiss Janey, Stacy tugged gently on her arm.

"Come on Janey."

Janey turned and kissed Brett on the cheek.

"So, Brett, can we still be friends? It's really important to me," she whispered.

Brett was hypnotized by the beautiful creature facing him. *Why does she have to leave now?*

"Uh sure. I'd like that," said Brett.

"Maybe we can talk later?" asked Janey.

After a few moments, he noticed that Janey had a questioning look as she waited for his answer. In spite of or because of Janey's effect on him, Brett was only able to nod.

"You're so sweet, Brett," said Janey with a hint of sexiness.

She was gone before Brett could do anything more.

He stood still in a stunned silence with music roaring around him. *We were just getting somewhere and now she's gone.* A heavy sadness enveloped him. *I don't want to just be friends. That's not enough.* His mind was filled with regret that he had not recognized her inner and outer beauty before. The date now seemed much different. He saw himself as an insensitive, clumsy, idiot. *I wonder if I even have a chance with her?*

As Brett dealt with self-doubt and heartache, Janey and Stacy approached the restroom. They started in.

"So, did you do what I said?" asked Stacy.

"Yeah, once I relaxed, it was easy."

"Well? Well?" asked Stacy.

"When I said I wanted to be friends, I don't think he wanted me to leave," said Janey.

"Now comes the hard part," said Stacy.

"I know, I know. Now, I make him chase after me," said Janey with a wistful look in her eyes. "I really liked that slow dance, though."

Just when Brett was going to seek out Janey again, Donny tapped him on the shoulder. He pulled Brett toward the back of the room where the music was not as loud.

"Wow, isn't this great? I have danced with some girls even," said Donny.

Brett was still sorting out his emotions about what had happened with Janey. He did not like having his thoughts interrupted but remembered that Donny might need some support. *Maybe a change will help me. This girl thing has turned me into jello.*

"Uh, good deal, Donny. Let's keep going around. Maybe you will dance and meet some more girls," said Brett.

"Yeah, yeah! Let's go," said Donny.

For Brett, the remainder of the night was a blur of music, dancing and frustration. He looked everywhere for Janey and Stacy but could not find them. *Dammit, where did she go? Did she leave already? It's like I saw the perfect wave coming at me but now it's gone.*

When the dance was almost over, Brett felt someone brush past him rubbing his shoulder. *What is that perfume I smell?* Before he could react, he was looking at Stacy and Janey walking briskly toward the exit. In a flash the gap between him and the girls was filled in with other teenagers leaving the dance. *Crap. There she goes.*

Chapter 37

The last song of the night was echoing through the hall when Brett found Donny talking to a pretty girl with long black hair.

"Are you ready to hit the road?" asked Brett.

"Give me a minute to get Mary's number," said Donny with a grin.

At least one of us is making progress, thought Brett.

They strolled out of the doors into the cool evening. A slight breeze was moving through the walkways and stars were sparkling bright overhead. Brett could still see the love of his life walking toward the parking lot, while Donny talked about what a great time he had.

"Yeah, I even got her number. Can you believe that?" asked Donny.

Suddenly, Brett saw Donny yanked violently to one side, and slammed into a small tree.

"Hey! What the…" Donny yelled.

Brett heard slapping sounds. Too late, he realized it was his head being pummeled by something or someone. He tried to lift his arms to protect himself but they were pinned at his side. A helpless feeling overcame him when he realized the defenseless position he was in. A hard blow crashed on his ear causing red sparks to spiral inside his head. Brett's knees became wobbly and unable to support him. He crumpled onto the sidewalk, still conscious, but stunned, in excruciating pain, and unable to see or think clearly. The right side of his head throbbed and he felt something wet trickling down from his nose.

Through a long, dark tunnel he heard a far-away voice gloating. "You got him good, Jimmy."

Another louder voice chimed in: "Get him up so I can fuck him up some more Freddy."

177

Brett thought he recognized the voice of his assailant but was not able to form his thoughts into a coherent image. There was a slight delay as he was being hoisted up, allowing him to find a little clarity. Three figures surrounded Brett. He knew one of the voices belonged to Jimmy Brooks. He also knew that he was in no shape to resist even one of his attackers. Enraged, Jimmy stood facing him.

"Not so tough now, are you, surfer boy!" he snarled.

Jimmy punched Brett repeatedly in the stomach and sides as the Freddy and Dusty easily held him in place. When Brett started to slip toward a dark abyss, Jimmy Brooks yelled at him.

"Now you'll see what happens to surfers who fuck with me."

"Yeah Jimmy, get him with the knife," screamed Dusty. "Fuck him up, Jimmy."

Suddenly, a high pitched scream pierced Brett's thick, inner fog, and everything around him transformed. He was released and plopped onto the hard cement. He looked at Jimmy Brooks, who seemed taller, wider and meaner than he remembered. Jimmy was yelling as he turned in circles, grabbing at his face. Something shiny flashed in the light and fell clattering on the sidewalk. As the scene unfolded, Brett was able to focus. He saw the source of the wild screaming and could not help smiling through the pain. Janey rode astride Jimmy's back with her long legs wrapped around his waist. Her fingers clawed at his face, eyes and hair.

"Get away from him you stupid creep! Leave him alone!" she screamed.

In Brett's dazed state, Janey seemed like an Amazon warrior destroying a hated enemy. He almost felt sorry for Jimmy, almost. Jimmy was already bleeding around his eyes, and clumps of his hair were on his shirt. He was frantic to get Janey away from him, but she was fearless, ferocious and enraged. Brett watched in disbelief as Jimmy crumpled to the ground. Janey hopped off and turned to face him. She glared at Jimmy, who sat still with his hands covering his face. Her eyes radiated hatred. Her blouse and nylons were ripped and torn. Her skirt was above her knees with the side zipper now in front, and clearly, she didn't care. Her entire body was coiled, ready to attack again, if necessary.

Now, Brett noticed a gigantic presence. A huge older teenager dressed in a purple T-shirt, tan Bermuda shorts and flip-flops held both Dusty and Freddy by an arm, banging them into each other like rag dolls. He had a competitive gleam in his eyes. Brett had never seen a teenager that huge or that strong. He seemed bigger than all three of his attackers. He towered over everyone.

"Little boys, isn't it time to go home?" he said with a confident smile.

Freddy and Dusty were only able to nod yes as they were roughly and repeatedly bounced into each other, reminding Brett of two wet towels being slapped together.

"Before you go, answer this question. Are you ever going to mess with Brett Sloan again?"

Brett's attackers shook their wobbly heads as they were roughly pushed down the sidewalk. They scurried away like frightened squirrels crossing a busy street. A small crowd had gathered to watch the fight, but now the powerful newcomer took charge.

"Hey everyone, it's all over now. So, you can go home and let this kid recover."

He picked up the knife and turned to Jimmy.

"Is this your knife?"

Jimmy turned his head away blinking his bloodied eyes. The huge stranger's arm flashed slapping the back of Jimmy's head.

"Ow! Yeah, it's my knife," he whined.

A massive hand grabbed Jimmy by the arm and shook him. All of the bones in his body moved in different directions and his head moved up and down like a bobble head doll.

"Look at me you slug. I know you have been trying to get Brett beaten up by your slimy buddies. If I ever hear about that happening again, I will beat you senseless. Do you understand?"

"Uh yeah. I got it. Let me go. Let me go," moaned Jimmy.

"I see you tangled with the wrong wildcat. That little girl sure gave you hell. Get out of here, and don't even look cross-eyed at Brett Sloan again. Do you understand?"

"Yeah, yeah, just don't hurt me anymore," whined Jimmy.

What little remained of the crowd dispersed, leaving Donny, Janey, Stacy, and the newcomer who held out his hand to Brett.

"Brett, how are you feeling? My name is Eric Burns. I am proud to meet you"

Brett whispered through a split lip, "thanks, I feel like crap. Why did you help me?"

"My little brother is Tommy Burns. You saved him from drowning. You're part of our family now. If anyone messes with you, they deal with me and my football buddies. And, I mean anyone. Do you need a ride home?"

"No, thanks, I came with Donny."

Eric put his arm around Janey's shoulder and grinned.

"One last thing Brett. Be nice to this girl. She went after Jimmy when you needed somebody most. If it wasn't for her that turd would have cut you up for sure."

Brett looked into Janey's eyes and started to cry softly as everything that had happened came rushing in. "I will," he said. "I definitely will."

Janey leaned over to hug Brett, and he felt an enormous, serene wave rushing into him. He smiled, and let himself be carried away by the healing tide.

Chapter 38

After a few days of extreme pain, Brett's wounds began to heal. The doctor had assured Ann that he would be fine, in spite of his appearance. Brett wanted to be alone in the security of his apartment home with his mother. The outside world seemed overwhelming. *I sure hope that this is the end of me getting beat up. At least Eric Burns and his friends are on my side.*

During the healing process, Brett never stopped thinking about what Janey had done. *She must really love me to fight like that.* As his health continued to improve, his loving emotions toward Janey increased. He knew now that they should be together, but when he saw her for the first time he wanted to be whole. Both she and Stacy had called numerous times but he was not ready to talk. He needed time to think about the next time he would see Janey and what he would say.

When Brett came home the night of the fight, Ann was extremely upset, but he had assured her that he hadn't started the fight, and that the other guys got the worst of it. The doctor's assessment also eased her mind somewhat. Luckily for Ann, Stacy and Janey had related the details of what took place. She knew that Brett would never tell her the whole story. Ann was relieved to hear that Eric Burns would watch out for her son. Even when Brett was feeling better, he surprised his mother by staying around the apartment, except to buy school supplies.

"Honey, why won't you talk to those sweet girls who keep calling?" asked Ann.

"Uh, I'm not into that now. I need to get my head screwed on straight first," said Brett.

"Stacy told me what happened. Don't you think you can at least say 'hi' or something? Her cousin helped you didn't she?"

"Let's not talk about this. I will deal with it in my own way."

A few days before the first day of school, Greg and Bobby Stephens returned from vacation. By that time, Brett was ready to talk to his friends. The brothers visited one afternoon when Ann was at work. After listening to Brett's retelling of the events at the dance and the fight, Greg spoke.

"So dude, a lot of wild stuff has happened to you. Jimmy is still an asshole but I doubt he will mess with you anymore," said Greg

"Yeah. That Eric Burns is one tough guy," said Brett.

"So, tell me again what happened with Janey. It sounds like you have changed your mind about her."

"Uh, yeah. It was like I never even saw how great she was before. It was like I woke up."

Greg and Bobby both smiled.

"Dude, I know the feeling. It sorta hits you all of a sudden. What are you going to do?" asked Greg.

"I'm still figuring that out. This is new for me."

"I'll tell you something Brett. With girls, it's always new and we are always figuring it out," said Greg.

~~~

By Monday morning, Brett was ready for his first day of school. He smiled when the honk came from the Stephens car outside.

"Bye Mom."

"Have a good first day honey. You look so handsome," said Ann as she kissed him goodbye.

Greg and Mrs. Stephens did most of the talking on the ride to El Segundo High School. Brett quietly listened. When they pulled up to the drop off area, Donny Head was waiting with a small group of people. Donny waved excitedly at Brett when he stepped out of the car. *I wonder what he wants*, thought Brett.

"I'll see you guys later. Thanks for the ride," said Brett to the Stephens brothers.

Donny ran over yelling "Brett, Brett!"

"Hi Donny. What are you so pumped up about?"

"Everybody is talking about the fight and you saving that kid from drowning! All the girls are wondering if you're going steady with Janey! Can you believe it?"

"I'm not that big of a deal. Relax," said Brett looking to the sky.

At that moment, Janey walked past with Stacy. They both glanced at Brett. He stopped listening to Donny. His eyes followed Janey until she and Stacy stopped. They stood talking and waiting. Donny continued to talk non-stop into Brett's un-hearing ears.

"Hey, Donny. Let's talk later. I have something to do."

"Uh okay, Brett," said Donny.

Brett turned and strode toward the two girls. Janey looked up with bright, electric eyes and a tense jaw. Stacy held on to her cousin's arm with anticipation.

"Here he comes," said Stacy.

Janey pulled her arm closer to her body and Stacy with it. Although it was warm, she shivered slightly and swayed as if blown by a strong wind. She could not keep her eyes away from Brett, as much as she wanted to appear composed. As Brett neared he seemed different to Janey. There was a forceful directness about him, as if he was focused on one goal and nothing else. She felt a strength emanating from him that made her feel safe and brave. Brett ignored Stacy as he stood directly in front of Janey who released her cousin's arm. Their eyes met and locked as if a line of hot, electric current connected them.

"Janey, I just wanted to say that I'm sorry. I should have talked to you. Please forgive me. You saved my life and I didn't even thank you," said Brett.

Janey moved a step closer to Brett with a look of compassion. All tension released from her as she smiled in relief. Hope animated her face.

"Uh, er, I didn't save you. I just reacted. I hated what they were doing to you," she said.

Brett eased closer to Janey. She remained in place.

"I've changed. I'm different now," said Brett

"Oh? Really?" asked Janey.

"I guess what I mean is. Uh, um, do you want to go out with me? Do you like me? Because, I like you."

Janey inched toward Brett until her lips were next to his ear. Brett had his arms around her before he knew what had happened. Janey pulled him close and held on tight.

"I really like you. I really do. I want to be with you," she whispered.

Brett turned to see Janey's tear-streaked face. Then he kissed her lightly on the lips.

"I want to be with you too."

Chapter 39

It was almost dark. Freddy and Dusty were scurrying along Highland Avenue with Jimmy not far behind. He carried two large bags. Each of them was grinning.

"This is fuckin' awesome. We get drunk on vino tonight," crowed Freddy.

"Shit yeah. And, we don't need to go down to the beach with those assholes," said Dusty.

They arrived at the construction site. Their favorite house was almost complete. The trio slithered into the crawl space and crawled through the dust. After lighting candles and situating themselves, they opened a gallon of wine. Jimmy passed around large plastic cups from a stack in one of the bags. After pouring he looked up with a greedy smile.

"Listen, we can start small. We'll sell some of this wine to little twerps and see how it goes. I told a few kids to come over soon," said Jimmy.

"What if everybody hears about it?" asked Dusty.

"I told them to only bring a few friends. I just want enough to pay for these bottles."

Jimmy was interrupted by a high-pitched voice at the crawl space entrance.

"Are you guys in there?" asked the voice.

"Yeah, what do you want?" Jimmy replied.

"I came for the wine. I have money."

Jimmy grabbed the bottle of open wine and scrambled over toward the voice causing dust to fill the confined space. Freddy and Dusty watched but kept silent. A young boy stuck his head in the hole when Jimmy was almost there.

"Is that you Jimmy?" he asked.

"Yeah, give me the cash and I'll pour you some wine."

In a flash, a huge muscular hand grabbed Jimmy's arm and yanked. Jimmy hit his head on a crossbeam. A deep gash opened on his forehead. A steady stream of blood poured out. The gallon of red wine fell on its side, gurgling onto the ground. Another arm grabbed Jimmy and he was forcefully pulled through the hole and onto the ground beside the house. Jimmy was dazed and in pain. Eric Burns and another huge football player stood over him. Eric turned and yelled behind him.

"We found Jimmy. Over here."

The same two plain-clothes detectives that had been at Jimmy's apartment, strolled up. Both were smiling.

"Thanks for helping us find him, Eric," said one of the detectives.

"Uh, no problem. We'll be going now. Bye Jimmy. Enjoy your visit to jail," said Eric.

The other detective turned to Jimmy whose face was bloody from the gash. He handed him a handkerchief.

"Well Jimmy. I guess you tripped and hit yourself?"

"Fuck you pig. You did that," snapped Jimmy.

"Sorry, it wasn't us. We were over there. Eric was nice enough to find you for us," said the man.

The other detective chimed in.

"You better assume the position, Jimmy. We're taking you in."

"Bullshit! For what?"

"Well it seems you pissed off a bunch of good citizens out there by telling them lies about some surfer named Brett something. They felt compelled to deal with him but found out later that you misled them."

"No way I fuckin' did anything."

"Those guys don't like being messed with, I guess. When they found out what you did, they remembered some information about you that they felt we would want to know. Like the jewelry you stole and the man you robbed on The Strand. We have a whole list of things to look at."

"No fuckin way they said that," said Jimmy.

The detective smiled as he cuffed Jimmy.

"Sometimes when guys are about to go to jail, they look for ways to break the fall. You know, they give information on unsolved cases and we go easy on them. Once they start talking, it's like a flood. Lately, all the information is leading to you."

Jimmy stared straight ahead and said nothing as they walked him to the car.

When they were gone Dusty and Freddy relit the candles. The wait had been nerve-wracking for them, but now they relaxed. Freddy grabbed the remaining bottle of wine and twisted the cap off. After drinking enough to feel it, they talked about what had happened.

"Man, I thought they were going to come in here too," said Dusty.

"Shit, they took him in. I never thought I'd see that. Not Jimmy. I'm just glad those fuckers didn't get us," said Freddy.

"I guess we won't see him for awhile."

A look of drunken understanding came over Dusty. He took another swig of wine. After thinking for awhile Dusty spoke.

"I guess it's just us, then. Oh well, shit happens."

Freddy took a large gulp of wine and poured more. Both of them lit up cigarettes. Freddy could not stop a sly grin from forming.

"Yeah, shit happens," he said.

Chapter 40

Brett stood in the middle of Kelp St. looking down at the Pacific Ocean. A swift, hot wind blew up his back, causing his T-shirt to billow, on its journey down the hill to the sea. In spite of the heat, his skin was covered with goose bumps. For a moment, he forgot that the school year had started and summer was over. To him it was the perfect summer day. Waves were rolling in with surfers riding them. But, these were not average or even above average waves. The sun glistened from them and the wind lifted them like an invisible hand, creating perfectly formed cylindrical shapes.

A delicate, watery mist rose from the curling tubes as they crashed down with machine-like precision. As one lone surfer dropped into a wave, Brett's heartbeat increased. He felt a physical, magnetic pull toward the beach and water below. It was a day like nothing he had ever seen, except in movies or his dreams. He ran into the apartment and quickly changed into swimming trunks. As he loped down the hill he thought, *can this be real?*

Sand was flying up from his feet as Brett ran across the beach. He stopped briefly, at the ocean's edge, to see who was in the water. Greg Stephens was riding a wave further down the shore. Brett sprinted toward him and shoved his surfboard into the water and dove in after it. He burst up out of the water to the roar of pounding surf and paddled out in a channel between breaking waves. The waves were large enough to be ideal for riding, but not big enough to be intimidating. When he was outside the whitewater and breaking surf he saw Bobby Stephens and paddled to him.

"Man, is this bitchin or what?" said Bobby.

"Unreal, totally unreal," said Brett grinning from ear to ear.

He sat on his board and watched. He felt like he had been transported to an ideal surfing paradise. He was in no hurry to paddle into a wave or do anything for that matter. He sat on the end of his surfboard with the tip pointed toward the cerulean sky and absorbed everything with heightened awareness. The sun, hot offshore winds and spray coming up from the crashing waves touched him in the depths of his soul. The combination of weather and surf conditions made all of the surfers feel as if they had been transported into another dimension. It was a dimension of relaxed energy where every person was in sync with the elements.

Greg was paddling out toward Brett.

"Dude. Are you going to surf or what," he asked.

"Uh, er, yeah. I just can't believe this day and these waves. It's like heaven," said Brett.

Brett looked toward the horizon for swells of water that would soon form into waves, but could see none. He again became meditative. All of his senses were open and receiving information from the world around him, making it fresh and effervescent. As he closed his eyes, flashing images began to pass across his inner vision. His summer was like a disjointed movie highlight reel. His stomach jumped when he remembered the tiny airplane free falling toward the sea below. He felt the oven-like heat of Palm Springs with his father and a pretty blond girl. He saw days of playing in the water and soaking up sun on the beach, flash by.

Then, it was as if a second reel of the same movie started. The first scene was at Disneyland where he met a shy girl with her gossipy cousin. He saw that girl transform at the beach, gaining in confidence while deepening her tan. Brett remembered being kissed by that same girl and the tears that followed. Then, he felt a wave of physical pain as fists came at him and saw the flash of a razor sharp knife. He smiled, reliving the moment when Janey fought for him against huge odds. Goosebumps covered his entire body. He forgot about the perfect day, with perfect waves as her face filled his mind. Her love washed over him like unending swells of water from the deepest sea.

"Dude, dude. Here it comes," yelled Greg Stephens.

Brett's mind snapped awake as his friends furiously paddled toward mounds of thick water, forming further out to sea. He slapped down his board and followed them, feeling the sucking pull of water toward the incoming swells. He just made it up the steep face of large overhead wave only to see five more lining up. He stroked toward the waves like a man possessed. When he neared the top of the next wave he pulled his board around and stroked once, with both arms, pushing into the steep, liquid slope in front of him. Ecstasy enveloped Brett Sloan as he raced into a perfect tube.

About The Author

George Matthew Cole lives in Burien,
Washington with his wife and dog.
After a long career in the computer
support field, he became interested in
writing while attending a creative writing
class at a local community college. His
first novel, "Colt O'Brien Sees The Light"
was published in 2009. "El Porto
Summer" is based on the author's
experiences as a teenager in El Porto,
California in the 1960s.

Find more information about George
Matthew Cole at his web site.

http://www.georgemcole.com

Made in the USA
Lexington, KY
11 November 2016